I0579553

THE

CARMELITE

PROPHECY

ALSO BY JENNI WILTZ

The Romanov Legacy: A Natalie Brandon Thriller

The Sinner's Bible: A Natalie Brandon Thriller

The Red Road

A Vampire in Versailles

I Never Arkansas It Coming

THE CARMELITE PROPHECY

A Natalie Brandon Thriller

Jenni Wiltz

Decanter Press
PILOT HILL, CALIFORNIA

Copyright © 2016 by Jenni Wiltz.
All rights reserved.

No part of this book may be used or reproduced in any manner
whatsoever without written permission except in the case of brief
quotations embodied in critical articles or reviews.

This is a work of fiction. Names, characters, businesses, organizations,
places, events and incidents either are the product of the author's
imagination or are used fictitiously. Any resemblance to actual persons,
living or dead, events, or locales is entirely coincidental.

Published in the United States by Decanter Press.
For information, contact:
publisher@jenniwiltz.com

Publisher's Cataloging-in-Publication Data
Wiltz, Jenni.
The carmelite prophecy / Jenni Wiltz.
227 p. ; 22 cm.
ISBN 978-1-942348-08-5 (pbk)
ISBN 978-1-942348-07-8 (eBook)
1. France — History — Revolution, 1789-1799 — Fiction.
2. France — Fiction. 3. Suspense Fiction.
4. Thrillers (Fiction). I. Title.
PS3623.I48C37 2016
813'.6 — dc23
Library of Congress Control Number: 2016917056

For Uncle Mike & Aunt Molly

CHAPTER ONE

other Marie-Aimée de Jésus held out the notice, delivered by special order of the Legislative Assembly. Printed on a sheet of flimsy tissue, the ink had bled in all directions. *Even the letters weep for what will come,* she thought.

Sister Léonie pulled the paper from her hand. Her gray eyes narrowed as she read it through. "They're evicting us? But why?"

They stood before the arched window in Marie-Aimée's cell. Its east-facing view had been designed to give a supplicant proof of God's glory during morning prayers. Today, though, the sun was just a clock, ticking away all the time they had left. "You know why," Marie-Aimée said.

"They're tired of waiting, aren't they?"

"You were always my best student."

The novitiate's hand fell to her side. "What will we do?"

Fight, she wanted to say. But with three hundred twelve souls in her care, she had more to think about than her principles. She sank into the chair beside her escritoire and buried her hands in the pleats of her heavy brown habit.

What the Assembly asked…it was impossible. They wanted her to abjure loyalty to the church in favor of a state that had imprisoned the anointed king, defied the pope, and failed to feed the starving populace any better than the old regime. Compliance would result in eternal damnation, she was sure of it. But rumors flew faster than crows, and every whisper spoke of terror, blood, and blades for those who refused to obey the order. Could she condemn these women to a martyr's fate? Were their lives more precious than an oath?

She looked at the girl standing beside her.

For ten years now, she'd watched and waited, wondering if Léonie's strange visions were a gift from God or the product of madness. There were times Léonie knew things it was impossible for a nineteen-year-old girl to know. When asked, the girl would only say that a voice in her head had told her.

None of the traditional means of punishment — raps on the wrist, fasting, a hair shirt — had changed her answers. By the time she'd given up on punishment, it was too late. The other women needed Léonie. They asked her where the best spot to plant a new rosebush was, or whether a beloved niece would ever find the time to write. Léonie and her voice were right too often to ignore. Outside these walls, they would brand her as a lunatic … or a witch.

But Léonie wasn't the only problem.

If the Assembly took possession of the nunnery, they would find the door hidden behind the tapestry on the far wall. If they opened the door, they would find ... no.

It could not be allowed.

Marie-Aimée glanced sideways at her novitiate. The girl's face was long and narrow, with a sharp chin and long-lashed eyes. She was beautiful when she smiled, but she rarely did so. Her hands were red and rough from working in the garden and the laundry. *What if...*

No.

That could not be allowed, either, if only for the girl's safety.

There had to be another way.

A breeze from the open casement teased the Assembly's declaration from Léonie's grip. It arced toward the door, then drifted back to rest against her feet. Marie-Aimée picked it up and sighed. "I remember many mornings like this one."

"Hot before sunrise?" Léonie said, pulling at the neck of her habit.

"And the only cool place was the schoolroom. Still, the other girls couldn't wait for lessons to end."

"Not me," Léonie said.

"No, not you," Marie-Aimée agreed. "Every time I dismissed the class, you stood up like a defeated gladiator. You loved history."

Léonie offered one of her rare smiles. "I still do."

"Then you know what happened the last time a government tried to divorce itself from the one true faith."

"King Henry VIII of England. He closed the monasteries and took everything they had." Léonie narrowed her eyes. "Is that why they're doing this to us?"

"The hearts of these men are closed to me, as are their minds."

"But we have nothing worth taking! No jewels, no plate, no relics."

"That is not entirely true," Marie-Aimée said, glancing at the tapestry across the room.

Léonie gasped. Then she clamped her lips shut and closed her eyes.

"I know that look," Marie-Aimée said softly. "Is your voice telling you something?"

"Yes."

"Is it my secret?"

Léonie shook her head. "He does not know it."

"He will." Marie-Aimée opened her mouth, but found she could not speak. Forty years of silence could not be easily overcome. Deep in her belly, a feeling of sickness rumbled like hunger and her fingers sought the comfort of the rosary beads at her waist. *Is this what You want from me?* she asked. *Is this why You sent her to me all those years ago?*

But there was no answer.

God wanted her to solve this problem on her own.

"Open your eyes," she said. When the girl obeyed, she reached out and took the younger woman's hands in hers. "What do you love most in all the world?"

Léonie's forehead wrinkled. "I don't understand."

"It isn't something you understand, my dear. It's something you feel. What does your heart tell you?"

"Nothing," Léonie said, pulling back her hands and wrapping them around her midsection. "I hear my own thoughts and I hear the voice, both of them, all the time. I feel mad enough without listening to a heart, too. Even if it said anything, I wouldn't listen."

Marie-Aimée nodded.

What made Léonie blessed also made her strange, despised by the people of her village and feared by her own parents. She'd hoped to teach Léonie to hide her thoughts, to better prepare her for life outside the nunnery. The poor girl didn't belong here. She had too much anger in her heart to surrender it to God. Her plan had always been to send Léonie back out into the world, with the hope that she might expend all that anger and return of her own free will. But neither of them was ready — they needed more time.

This revolution was a disaster for them all.

Still, she had to try.

Marie-Aimée looked up at Léonie. "Have I ever told you where I was born?"

"Why should that matter?"

"I am from Reims," she said, rising to her feet. "The place where our kings are crowned and anointed by God. The place Clovis was baptized by Saint Remi, with chrism brought to him by the dove of the Holy Spirit. The place Jeanne d'Arc took from the English so that Charles VII might be crowned. There is no place more holy in all of France."

"So you love Reims above all."

"I love my city, yes, but now you know what it means when I say I love God more." She put her hand on the girl's shoulder. "What do you love most in all the world?"

Léonie closed her eyes. Marie-Aimée watched her sway, wondering what angels or demons held court inside the girl's head.

I'm the one who is mad, she thought, *trusting a girl who claims to have no heart.*

When Léonie opened her eyes, the pale gray orbs glimmered with tears. "The voice told me to say I love him. My head told me to say I love this place. But my heart told me it is you I love above all else." She sniffed and shook her head. "I have no conception of God outside this place, and no conception of a mother who isn't you. If God is love, then when I say I love you and I love this place, that must mean I love God, too."

Marie-Aimée kissed the girl's forehead. Suddenly, she felt old and tired and unequal to the task before her. *Let it be done,* she thought. "You saw the Assembly's order. You know how little time we have. There are things I must tell you before they come for us. Things you must know in case I do not survive."

Léonie gasped and stepped away. "Who would want to harm you? That's not how it happened in Henry's day."

"We are not in Henry's day, my dear."

"The voice says…" Léonie put her hands to her temples and grimaced. "The voice says we are not in Henry's day, but Mary's. Bloody Mary, who burned those who did not share her faith."

"I fear it is so." It hurt her to think of this girl, intelligent and strange, being at the mercy of the Assembly and the mob it pretended to rule. "There are things I must call upon you to do for me in the coming days. Trust me when I tell you they are more important than anything else, even our lives. Are you ready to do what is necessary?"

"I don't know," Léonie said, taking a step back. "What must I do?"

"I know you're afraid," she said. "I am, too. But we must put aside our fear, like Daniel in the lions' den. God will protect us as long as we do His work." She walked to the other side of her escritoire and opened the widest drawer. The knife, when she drew it out, trailed thin cobwebs and sprinkles of dust.

She carried it to Léonie's side and placed it in her hand, closing the girl's fingers around the handle. "Are you ready to do what is necessary?"

CHAPTER TWO

JANUARY 2006
PARIS, FRANCE

Evrard *Baptiste surveyed* the cemetery. Bordered by a chain-link fence and surrounded by multi-story housing projects, it had none of the charm of Père Lachaise or Montparnasse. It was a place to put people no one would remember.

He could use that.

His footsteps crunched on the gravel pathway as he stepped toward one of the grave sites. In front of that grave knelt a man about ten years younger than him. Tall and broad-shouldered, the man had a deep tan and short blond hair. He was out of uniform, dressed in a nylon jacket and jeans.

"*Bonjour,*" Baptiste said.

The kneeling man turned his head. His reflective sunglasses showed Baptiste the mass of clouds gathering in the distance and his own mane of wiry hair. When he spoke, his voice was deep and raw. "Who are you?"

"Doctor Evrard Baptiste." He paused, but the other man made no sign of recognition.

"What are you doing here?"

"The same thing you are."

"I doubt that." The man turned back to the raised granite tomb, unadorned with a cross, dates, or a name. "How do you even know who's in there?"

"I know," Baptiste said softly. He stepped alongside the tomb, dragging his gloved fingers across the surface. "Were you ashamed of him?"

The other man rose. "I asked who you are."

"And I asked if you were ashamed that a hero of France lies beneath that cold stone without a name to remind the world of his existence."

"That's not what you said."

Baptiste smiled. "My mistake." He put his hands in his coat pockets and turned to look at the housing projects. A cold wind blew the tails of his scarf over his shoulder. "You came late in his life, didn't you?"

"By necessity." The other man widened his stance and folded his hands behind his back. "Did you serve with him?"

"I am a civilian."

"I meant in prison."

Baptiste glared at him. "When they told de Gaulle about the generals' revolt, he was in the theater, watching Racine's *Britannicus*. Did you know that?"

The blond man made no acknowledgement of the question or his answer.

"Of course you don't," he said softly. "Britannicus was the son of Emperor Claudius. He should have been his father's heir, but Claudius's stepson, Nero, took the throne instead. The boy did not live long afterward. By all accounts, he was bright and well-liked. His only crime was being inconvenient for those with more ambition and fewer scruples. Does that sound familiar?"

"What do you want from me?"

"De Gaulle abandoned Algeria. He abandoned every French citizen born there, despite the rights and protections our constitution promised them. When your father and the generals tried to stop him, he abandoned them, too." He glanced up at the younger man. "De Gaulle was afraid to fight the Muslims. He was afraid of their bombs and their guerrilla warfare. Afraid of their desert and their language." He paused. "Chirac was afraid, too. The bomb that killed your father was the first of how many ... four?"

"Seven," the man answered. "If you count the ones that didn't go off."

"It was a tragedy that should have been met with force instead of fear. But not everyone is afraid."

The other man peeled off his sunglasses. His eyes were the color of petrified amber, all emotion fossilized beneath their surface. "Are you?"

"No man who knows our history should be afraid. Who did Charles Martel defeat at the Battle of Tours? From whom did Charlemagne seize the islands of Corsica and Sardinia? Who did Napoleon destroy at the Battle of the Pyramids? For more than a thousand years, we have fought to protect our land and our faith from the threat of Islam. Now the powers that be cannot even stop teenagers from lighting cars on fire."

The other man curled his lip. "They never found the man who planted the bomb on my father's train."

"They didn't want to. They would rather people forget." Baptiste paused. "But I found him."

"Tell me where." His right hand fell to his hip, reaching for a weapon that wasn't there.

"You are a Légionnaire, like your father before you."

"Not like him," the other man said softly. "Not yet."

"France needs men like you. And she needs someone to lead them."

"Is that your way of telling me who you are?"

Baptiste felt his heart beat faster. This was the moment it all began. "Do you want to mourn your father or do you want to avenge him?"

"Are you offering me a job?"

"A chance," Baptiste said. "The benefits are better than the pay."

The other man paused. He curled his lip, then stepped backward. One hand slid into his pocket and he pulled out a centime, which he twirled up and over each finger. "My father used to take me to the Fontaine des Innocents every Sunday. He would twirl a coin, just like this, until I pulled it out of his hand and tossed it into the fountain. You've spent our lunch money, he would say. So I always wished for more money." He sighed. "I should have wished for more time with him."

"He was sent to prison for his willingness to fight the Muslim rebels in Algeria. Then he was taken from you by a Muslim coward who thought planting a bomb would help create an Islamic state in Algeria. I cannot give you back the time he lost, or the time you lost with him. But I can give you the opportunity to take that time from others."

"What is this thing you want to do?"

"We will find people like us. We will educate them ... and we will arm them. There are skills you can teach that we will need when the time is right."

"And you'll tell me where that man is, the one who planted the bomb?"

"I'll take you to him now." Baptiste smiled. "Consider it a signing bonus."

The man placed his hand flat on the tomb. "He wanted me to be a priest. Did you know that?" Then he splayed his fingers, releasing the centime he'd clutched between them. It rolled and rounded to a stop at the head of the granite slab. "The day I buried him, I burned his Bible and went to the Légion's recruiting office. I spent more time escorting diplomats in the Côte d'Ivoire than killing mujahideen."

"There will be no diplomats this time," Baptiste said. "But I do have one condition of employment." When the younger man turned his head, he said, "Put your father's name on that tomb."

The other man stood up and put on his sunglasses. "When do we start?"

CHAPTER THREE

"*It's official,*" *Beth* Brandon said, flinging her leather tote into a chair. "We just survived a near-death experience." She collapsed onto the queen-sized bed, arms laid out in the shape of a cross.

"I liked it," Natalie said, moving toward the hotel room's third-story window. She pushed aside the filmy curtain liner and looked out over the angular rooftops of Paris. The cab driver had taken them from Orly to the Marais in record time, with complete disregard for speed limits, traffic signs, and according to her sister, human life. Their hotel, a rectangular building enclosing a cement courtyard, had wrought-iron balconies painted bright turquoise. The floor squeaked in four places walking from the door to the window.

Natalie touched the glass with her nose. Her eyes, too pale a blue to darken her reflection, glanced from spire to rooftop to dome. She wanted to go exploring, but knew she'd have to wait for Beth. She couldn't go out alone in a new city, alone, with only Belial for company.

"Are you hungry?" Beth asked.

Natalie shrugged.

"Is Belial behaving?"

"So far," she said, looking south toward the Seine. A whisper of movement behind her eyes unleashed a flood of goosebumps under her T-shirt. "But the alprazolam is wearing off. He's starting to breathe again."

Beth pulled back a cashmere sleeve to glance at her watch. "I need to check in at the venue and have them run through my slides. If I leave now, I can get back in time for dinner. You think you can wait that long?"

"I could wait forever," Natalie said, perching on the windowsill. The peaked roofs, embellished corners, and laundry lines strung across courtyards looked like the setting of an urban fairytale. In San Francisco, from her apartment on the corner of Valencia and 26th, she mostly saw power lines, pigeons, and people who sucked at parallel parking.

"You have what you need?" Beth asked.

"It's in my bag."

Beth grabbed Natalie's canvas messenger bag and brought it to her. "Just in case," her sister said, unlatching the flap to reveal a dozen airport-sized liquor bottles.

Natalie reached for her sister's hand. "Thank you for bringing me. I know it would have been easier if you didn't."

Beth folded her into a hug and Natalie breathed in the warm, golden scent of her sister's perfume. "Everything that happens, good and bad, we're in it together, remember?

We've gone through too much to change that now. Besides, I wouldn't have missed this for the world."

Belial stirred and shifted his wings. The movement sent tentacles of pain coiling deep behind her eyes. *Me neither,* the angel said.

Natalie reached for one of the bottles in the messenger bag.

"Already?" Beth said softly.

"He's talking now." Natalie unscrewed the cap and tilted the plastic bottle to her lips. The rye whiskey burned a peppery trail from tongue to stomach.

Belial made a noise like thunder, letting it rumble in his throat. *You don't want to do that. We'll be going out soon.*

"No," she said. "I'm waiting here for Beth."

"You tell him." Beth squeezed her hand. "Pick out something we can go see tonight, okay?" She grabbed the makeup bag from her suitcase and headed for the bathroom.

Natalie screwed the cap onto the empty bottle. It had all happened so fast — the call, and then the trip. First, Beth's dean at the university had gone in for emergency gallstone surgery. As they wheeled him into the OR, the department secretary had called and asked Beth to take his place at a conference in Paris on four days' notice. Beth had scrambled to familiarize herself with his paper ("Going out as a Ghazi: Latin and Arabic Depictions of Faith, Weaponry, and Destiny in the Battle of Tours"), make some slides, bribe the neighbor to babysit Seth, and ... figure out what to do with her.

I can't be left alone for three goddamn days, she thought. What kind of person can't be trusted for three days?

You, little one, Belial answered.

Natalie took a deep breath and looked out over the city. As part of her cognitive therapy, Beth had taught her to run through facts, names, numbers, and dates when she felt overwhelmed or on the verge of losing control. It was easier when Beth quizzed her, bombarding her with questions like those machines that shot tennis balls at people who had no one to play with. But here, the city itself bombarded her with questions. Every glance revealed another place where something had happened, where someone had lived and breathed and died and seen things only described in history books.

I can do this, she thought.

Just a few blocks southeast was the Place de la Bastille. Although there was nothing left of the building itself, the spot marked the location of the infamous prison.

"The Bastille," she said, closing her eyes.

For as long as she could remember, facts and numbers had come easily to her. Once she read them in a book or heard them spoken aloud, they stayed in her brain. Retrieving them and getting them past Belial was another story.

"Attacked on July 14, 1789." She paused as the calculation whirred in her head. "A Tuesday. There were seven prisoners inside: four forgers, two nut jobs, and a count. Ninety-eight attackers killed, plus seven garrison members and the governor. Lafayette mailed the key to George Washington as a token of respect."

Interesting choice, Belial said. *But that's not where we're going.*

"We're not going anywhere," she said, pulling a second bottle from her bag. "I told you that already." She chugged the contents, feeling a heady warmth spread through her chest.

You know you're destroying your liver, don't you?

"Not fast enough," she said.

The angel, perched in the space between her brain and her skull, was not a fan of alcohol. It was the only thing that slowed him down and let her out-think him. Beth preferred therapy, but even she admitted that the fastest, easiest way to get Belial to shut up was to drink him into silence.

The bathroom door squeaked against the uneven floor as Beth emerged, lipstick reapplied. Thin, blonde, and blue-eyed, Beth had given birth without drugs, run a marathon, made pie crust from scratch, published three books, and given the university's graduation commencement speech. The fact that she still threw up before every speaking engagement made Natalie smile. Her sister was human after all.

"You're not even speaking today," she said as Beth dropped her makeup bag back into her suitcase. "What's with the nerves?"

"It's a meet-and-greet in a language I barely speak with guys I quoted in my dissertation. Five bucks says I hurl all over Evrard Baptiste's shoes."

"They know you're not presenting your own research, right?"

"That's the only reason I agreed to do it." Beth shivered. "I need a new specialty. Russia still gives me nightmares."

Natalie bit her lip. *Me too,* she thought, remembering everything that had happened after Beth's book on Nicholas II came out. The tsar's missing treasure had almost gotten them killed... but it had also shown her that it was possible to love someone other than her sister or her nephew.

Constantine, she thought, wishing he were with her. But he was still in Moscow, visiting his parents and his sister, Lana. She had to be patient.

"I know what makes nightmares go away," she said, reaching into her bag and holding out one of the plastic bottles.

Beth shook her head. "Those are yours."

"Beth, you'll be gone all of what…two hours? I'd pass out if I drank all these."

"I feel weird leaving you in a strange place. We just got here. What if Belial—"

"I'll be fine," Natalie said. "I can do this."

"Battles of the Hundred Years' War, in order, beginning with Crécy. Go."

"Beth. You're stalling."

"Shit." Her sister bit back a grimace. "I think I'm gonna throw up again."

"You're not. Just go. I'm fine, I promise."

"Think about what you want to eat tonight, okay?" Beth grabbed her tote and leaned her head against the doorframe. "Just one," she said softly.

It was a promise they'd made to each other after Russia: just one more smile, one more try, one more gasp of hope, one more breath, when everything else had gone wrong. "Just one," Natalie replied, smiling until Beth closed the door.

Finally, Belial said. *I thought she'd never leave.*

"Fuck off," she said, unscrewing the cap of the bottle she'd offered Beth.

There is a great evil in this place.

"There's evil everywhere."

Evil doesn't die, little one. It can be neither created nor destroyed.

"Did you whisper that in Newton's ear, too?"

She turned her head toward the window. Suddenly, there were no people visible at all — no women watering geraniums in a planter box, no kids leaning out a window to smoke while their parents weren't home. "What do you want from me?"

There is someone I want you to meet.

"Not gonna happen."

Two people, actually.

"Let it go."

What if I told you there were things here, places here, that carry a part of your bloodline?

"I wouldn't give a shit. Beth is the genealogy freak, not me."

Don't lie to me, little one. I'm a part of you, remember?

She reached for another plastic bottle. "Whiskey," she said. "Whiskey's about to be a part of me."

Belial tapped her with the tip of a wing. The lightning bolt of pain made her drop the tiny bottle. *If I made it sound like you have a choice, then I am sorry.*

She pressed her hands to her temples, trying to fight the pounding inside. "I'm waiting for Beth. I don't want to go anywhere without her."

I need you, little one.

Tears of pain squeezed from behind her closed eyelids. "I don't need you."

This affliction you believe me to be...do you think you are the only one to have it? It has marked your family many times before.

It skipped your sister, but who might it strike in the next generation?

"Seth," Natalie whispered. Her nephew was still in grade school. He knew nothing about the evil of the world and she wanted to keep it that way as long as possible. "You promised you'd leave him alone."

I promised and I obey, little one. But I am not the only one you need to worry about.

This was her nightmare, one she never seemed to be able to wake from — a future where Beth or Seth or Constantine got hurt because of her. Because of something a power beyond her control had brought upon them. "If something threatens Seth, swear to me you'll fight for him against anything, living or dead. Promise me that, and I'll do what you want."

With all the power bestowed on me, I will protect your sister's child if you come with me now.

She dropped the empty plastic bottle onto the floor. "Let's go."

CHAPTER FOUR

here was no knock. No message. Not a single word of warning to tell the three hundred twelve frightened girls under her care that the deputies from the Assembly had come to administer the oath.

Mother Marie-Aimée heard the creaking and splintering of the abbey's oaken doors as the deputies smashed their way through. She sat up in bed, clutching her heart. "It has begun," she whispered.

In an instant, she heard shrieking from the ground floor below her cell.

The angry voices of the deputies outside.

The clang of irons.

The crash of crockery swept to the floor.

She ignored all of it. Sleeping in her habit had become a necessity as this moment neared, and she slipped from bed fully clothed. As she opened the door to her cell, Sister

Léonie came running toward her. "*Ma mère*," she said, gray eyes wide with terror. "What are we —"

"It is time," Marie-Aimée said, pulling the girl into her cell and closing the door. She wrapped Léonie in a fierce embrace and kissed her forehead. "You know what to do."

Slowly, two thin arms encircled her waist. "I'm frightened."

"So am I, my dear. May God give us strength." Marie-Aimée squeezed the girl's hands. Then she flung open the chest at the foot of her bed and lifted out the tunic and cowl of a Carmelite monk. The girl slipped it over her chemise, wound the leather cincture around her waist, and reached for her rosary.

"Wait," Marie-Aimée said. Her fingers slid to her own cincture and removed the string of polished silver beads. "This was given to me by Pope Clement, blessed by his very hand. Take it and keep it safe."

"But what about —"

Marie-Aimée closed the girl's shaking fingers over the silver and pried the wooden rosary from her other hand. "No questions," she said, when Léonie opened her mouth to protest.

Finally, the girl obeyed, smoothing the brown wool over her legs. "Like the cross," she mumbled. "Like the soil."

Marie-Aimée raised the cowl over Léonie's shorn hair. "Like a man." She stepped back to glance at her handiwork. The girl looked young and frightened, but not immediately identifiable as a young and frightened nun.

Marie-Aimée hurried to the far wall. "Our Father, who art in heaven," she whispered, pulling back the tapestry that helped warm the rough limestone in winter.

In the courtyard below, she heard hooves clop on cobbled stone, pulling wheels that squeaked and bumped toward their door.

"Hallowed be thy name." Barely visible in the hundred-and-seventy-year-old masonry was a rectangle, half the height of a man, outlined by a parchment-thin gap in the mortar. She pressed her entire body weight against its left side, swiveling the secret door open.

Léonie scuttled into the blackness, clutching the silver rosary to her chest. When she turned for one last look, her chin quivered like leaves in an autumn wind.

"Be brave, *ma fille*," Marie-Aimée said. "We will always dwell together in the house of the Lord. I am there, in your heart, when you need me."

Something crashed in the hall outside the door to her cell.

Marie-Aimée looked back to the weeping girl. "Do not come out for any reason, do you understand?"

Léonie nodded. Tears traced waterfalls down her dusty cheeks.

"Never forget who you are and what I have taught you."

"But I don't know who I am," the girl sobbed.

"You are the daughter of my heart."

A crash against her door splintered the bolt.

"Thy kingdom come," she said, pushing the right side of the door to swivel it shut. Her last glimpse was of Léonie's stormy eyes and determined chin, one hand raised in a lonely farewell.

"Thy will be done." She slid the tapestry back into place and hurried to her door, flinging aside the shattered bolt.

A man with long hair in a dirty chemise and striped trousers waited for her. He held up his hands, dangling a set of leg irons.

On earth as it is in heaven, she thought.

The man grabbed her arm and hauled her out of her cell. She looked over the railing into the foyer below. Deputies dragged girls into the courtyard, where she'd heard the horses arrive a moment ago. *Carts*, she thought. *Irons.*

The men had come prepared. A smile curled her lips. *They knew we would not swear.*

She jerked her arm out of the deputy's grip. "I am the Reverend Mère Marie-Aimée de Jésus de l'Église Saint-Joseph-des-Carmes. It is your duty in the eye of God and the republic you serve to treat these women with care and respect."

The man's brandy-soaked breath made her eyes water. "It is my duty," he said, "to administer the oath of loyalty to our glorious republic. Whether you swear it or not, we are ordered to take possession of this building."

Two men dragged one of the older nuns, Sister Marie-Henriette de la Providence, into the courtyard, her bare feet trailing on the ground behind them. "What have you done to her?" Marie-Aimée shouted.

Behind her, one of the men upstairs shouted for help. "Come on, boys," he said. "Time to find those trunks of gold!"

"There are no earthly riches here," she said to the long-haired man before her. "We feed the poor. We give everything we have to them."

"That's what the Benedictines said. Then we found chalices and plates of gold in the monks' quarters." He drew a finger across his throat. "They don't need 'em now."

Give us this day our daily bread. She was glad her voluminous habit hid the shiver that shook her from head to toe. "All this is to raise funds for the army, is it not, monsieur? The Assembly could have asked for our help. We are the brides of Christ, but we were all born French."

"Asked?" he said. "All those tithes, all those years of taking francs from those who could least afford it, and you want us to ask for it back?" He reached back and slapped her across the face. "I am a citizen of France and you will address me as such."

Marie-Aimée's head snapped backward, black spots dancing before her eyes. Three nuns rushed forward, but the men barred their way with raised bayonets and pikes. "Don't hurt them," she said.

"I'd be more worried about what we're going to do to you."

"You can't hurt me," she said. Out of the corner of her eye, she saw two men atop the staircase enter her cell. *No, she* thought. *Get out of there. The girl needs more time.*

There was only one thing to be done.

Marie-Aimée sighed. She stood as straight as she could and walked toward the abbey's splintered door. *And forgive us our trespasses as we forgive those who trespass against us.*

"Where are you going?" the man said.

"You came to administer my oath, did you not? I wish you to do so in the courtyard, in full view of God and all the men you brought to this place with evil and sin in their hearts."

A flood of protests from the captive women echoed against the high stone ceiling, but Marie-Aimée held out her hands. "Don't be afraid," she called to them. "I have nothing but love in my heart for God and how He has allowed me to serve Him in this life."

"Don't do this," said Sister Marie-Joseph, reaching a hand past one of the deputies.

Marie-Aimée clasped it quickly as she passed. *And lead us not into temptation, but deliver us from evil.*

"All right," the deputy said. "If that's how you want to do it." He clapped his hands and raised his voice. "Come and see, boys, come and see! The old lady wants to give you a show."

It took every ounce of willpower she had not to turn her head and look over her shoulder as she stepped into the courtyard. She winced when her bare feet stepped on gravel and splinters, strewn over the cobblestones by the waiting carts' rickety wheels.

The deputies had arranged their horses and carts in a half circle around the abbey's entrance. One of the horses snorted, jerking his head against the reins. The carts had handfuls of straw spread over their rough floors. She knew why.

For thine is the kingdom and the power and the glory.

She stopped in the center of the half circle and turned to face the deputy. A noise in her ears buzzed like a swarm of bees. It took her a moment to realize it was the sound of her heart, beating wildly with a fear that threatened to swallow her. Behind the deputy, his men followed with nervous smiles on their faces. Some of them pushed the nuns along before them.

They crowded to fill in the other half of the circle as the deputy walked up to her. He pulled a piece of paper from his pocket and unfolded it slowly. "Do you swear," he read, pausing to grin at his men. "Swear to uphold the constitution of the republic of France, abjuring all other entities that may claim earthly sovereignty over the decrees and orders hereof?"

Her eyes drifted over the faces of the women God had brought into her care. *Help them*, she prayed. *Save them.* She swallowed the sob in her throat. Many of them were going to die here with her ... because of her. That was the hardest to bear. Not letting go of this life, not the pain that was surely coming. *I'm sorry*, she wanted to say.

Marie-Aimée looked the deputy in his eyes. "No," she said.

Before he could silence her, she looked out again at the women. "Make your own choice. Be free in your heart, wherever it leads you. If you have truly accepted God, He will guide you to the right decision. Your sisters will not judge you. These men will judge you, but as they do unto us, God will do unto them."

The deputy nodded and folded his piece of paper.

He held out his right hand and one of the deputies handed him a rifle. He slid the folded sheet over the point of the bayonet and thrust it into her belly.

"God bless you," she said.

One of the sisters shrieked. Another sobbed. She saw them turn to each other, foreheads to shoulders, hands over eyes.

The deputy pulled out the blade and stabbed her again, jerking it downward to force her to the ground.

She fell.

Now and forever.

The orange sun rose high over the abbey walls. She looked up at it, feeling its warmth on her face and in her belly. The last thing she saw as the lids of her eyes fluttered shut was a small white face peering out from her cell.

Amen.

CHAPTER FIVE

The medallion was warm in his hands. The raised outline of an oliphant, a medieval horn made of an elephant's tusk, was still sharp. The leather cord slotted through the hole in the top had thinned over the years and would need replacing soon. Once this job was done, there would be time for small repairs.

Evrard Baptiste set the medallion aside and reached for his laptop.

Of the three courses offered in August – Leatherwork, Swordmaking, and Armor – the second had the most sign-ups. His students had screen names like VertGallant88 or DeMolay_Vendredi13. They were office workers, bureaucrats who wanted to brag that they'd made a sword on their summer vacation, while their co-workers got sunburned in Cavalaire-sur-Mer. The real students returned after dark, however, when he taught them how to make weapons of a different sort. If a few students showed up the next morning with dark circles under their eyes and strange burns on their fingers, no one noticed. And no one noticed when those students slipped on a simple medallion and took their caches back to Lille, Marseilles, or Arromanches.

Ten years later, there were six hundred former students waiting for him to give the command. Six hundred students trained in weaponry and street fighting by former Légionnaires, men and women whose fathers and grandfathers had died to protect France's settlers in Indochina and Algeria.

The Fourth Republic had betrayed those men.

The Fifth Republic had betrayed all of France, allowing terrorists to rule her streets.

The time to act was near.

Six hundred organized and simultaneous attacks on mosques was newsworthy. Six hundred organized and simultaneous attacks on mosques led by a decorated native son wielding the most important relic in French history was a revolution.

Baptiste picked up his medallion and turned it over. The image struck onto the back was a woman's face, eyes tilted to the sky with tears streaming down her face.

Marianne.

The mythical woman who represented his country, under attack every day from the terrorists and the immigrants and the spineless government that allowed them to destroy the fabric of a nation that had once bent Europe to its will. "I will not fail you," he said, resting the pad of his index finger on her cheek.

He was no longer alone in his quest, either.

That morning, the commander of the 6ᵉ Light Armored Brigade had pledged his support. That included the 13ᵉ Demi-Brigade de Légion Étrangère, the only body of the Foreign Legion to resist Vichy's control during World War II. If they were with him, he knew the sons and grandsons of the men who had fought at Bir Hakeim would follow. He'd been hoping for the whole of the 3ᵉ Division, with its biological and chemical weapons expertise, but he knew how to be patient. They would do as he asked once they knew the 6ᵉ was on his side.

There was only one thing missing.

He picked up the burner phone and texted Maillard. *Sight confirmation requested.*

Ten seconds later, his phone buzzed with Maillard's response. *10m. Maybe less.*

His fingers flew over the keys. *Bring her to me now.*

CHAPTER SIX

The gate at 72 Rue de Vaugirard was open. The façade of an ochre-colored church rose behind a limestone perimeter wall, topped with a triangular cornice and faceless carvings of saints. A courtyard of cobblestones led from the gate to the church.

Natalie looked up at the spire, its thin cross ornamented with lacy filigree work. "Is this where we're going?"

Belial shivered. There was a coldness inside him, something she'd never felt before. She was used to his anger and scorn, even a few rare moments of tenderness, but not this. It was as if the angel inside her was afraid.

She tugged on the long sleeves of her T-shirt. The walk from the hotel had taken an hour, and she'd pushed them up when she started to sweat in the late afternoon sun. The bright light had made the long, puffy scars on her forearms tingle. She would never have revealed them at home, but here in Paris, she knew they'd never be the most interesting thing for others to stare at.

She smoothed the wrinkled cotton over her wrists. "Why are we here, Belial?"

Go through the wooden door, little one.

Natalie blinked. "I'm standing in front of an open gate."

The entrance to the chapel is through the wooden door.

She stepped back from the gate and glanced down the street. A few feet further down, cut into the walls surrounding the church, was an entrance with two wooden doors. They were taller and narrower than any doors she'd seen in San Francisco, so different from the dark rounded doors of Mission Dolores. A faded plaque above them read "Entrée de la Chapelle."

The door on the left was open.

She stepped toward it and glanced over her shoulder. On the ground floor of the building behind her, a florist's shop had already closed for the day. A pharmacy's sliding door opened to admit a small woman with white hair. Above the shops, four uniform stories of windows, iron balconies, and white shutters faced the church. Its dome reflected in one of the second story's windows, centered between a shutter and the window frame. It was a postcard moment, framed perfectly, but she felt the angel shiver again.

Go inside, little one.

"I don't want to," she said. "I should have waited for Beth."

You promised.

"Why does this place scare you?"

It will tell you who you are.

Suddenly, she heard the echo of a female voice in the darkest corner of her mind, a place only Belial had ever seen: *Whatever I have done that was good, I have done at the bidding of my voices.*

"Who is that?" she shrieked, spinning to face the street behind her.

A man walking into the pharmacy shook his head at her.

"Belial, who was that? What are we doing here?"

Find the shrine in the Salle des Épées and I will show you.

§

The room was labeled "Rangement," which didn't sound anything like what Belial had called it. It had an ordinary door, with the fading glow of natural light shining through the cracks in the frame. She knew it was the right place when Belial began to shake. "What's in there?" she asked, reaching for the knob.

Evil, the angel replied.

Her hand froze.

Go inside, Belial said. *Now.*

Natalie glanced behind her, down the dark hallway and staircase that led down to the church and courtyard. "I want to go back," she said.

It's too late for that now, Belial answered.

He flicked her with a wing and she gasped in pain as she pushed open the door.

The room was small, with polished wood flooring and plastered walls. Its only window opened onto the gardens behind the church. A glass-fronted box stood against the wall on her right. A gray sculpture of the Madonna and Child kept watch beside it. The Virgin was missing her right hand and the Christ child his right foot. She wondered if, somewhere in France, someone had the Virgin's hand on a coffee table.

To the left of the box was an etched portrait of a nun, La Rev. Mère Marie-Aimée de Jésus, according to the inscription. A second frame sat on the right, its contents turned to face the wall like a disobedient child. Frayed wires above both frames indicated they had been hung at one time.

That is not a box, Belial said.

She stepped toward it. Narrow and rectangular, it rose as high as her chest. Someone had painted it the color of eggshells, as if the contents were being incubated. A slender tree branch rested across its top. Dozens of faded leaves had fallen to the floor.

It's an offering, she realized. She knelt and pulled out three strands of long brown hair, dropping them onto the floor.

That's when she saw it.

The glass front revealed a piece of an older, unplastered wall. Two thick cuts gouged the stone, each longer and wider than her finger. Rivulets of dried blood trailed beneath them, tiny waterfalls running from abdomen to floor.

Without touching it, she felt cold. "Is this what you wanted me to find?"

Belial moaned, a wordless lament that vibrated behind her eyes.

"Whose blood is this?"

Yours, the angel answered. *And mine.*

The scars on her arms began to itch, as if the sight of dried blood reminded them of how they'd come to be. She'd done it for Beth, to try and give her sister the life she should have had. Part of her would always wish she'd succeeded. Just by being here, she was proving her own point — she was a terrible sister and a terrible person.

She looked at her reflection in the glass. Her first instinct was to break it, break all of it, break the glass and use the pieces to break the skin that held her broken soul together. Why hadn't she been brave enough to tell Belial no? Why couldn't she have suffered on the floor of the hotel room, screaming if she had to, until Beth came back?

I'm weak, she thought. *Beth would have wanted me to be strong.*

"Whose blood is this?" she asked again.

Let me show you.

The angel flicked his wings and fire-bright bolts of pain exploded behind her eyes. Natalie sucked in her breath and fell to her knees. A drop of sweat rolled into her eye and stung it with salt. She closed it and wiped her forehead with her hand, but when she opened her eyes, everything had gone black. It was Belial, clamping down on her optic nerve.

"I made a mistake," she whispered. "I don't want to know. Belial, take me back to the hotel."

The angel didn't answer her.

"I hate you," she said, reaching out with splayed hands. She felt the surface of the shrine beneath her fingertips, all cold glass and slick paint. She moved her hands to the right, feeling for the smooth plaster of the wall. Sliding one hand over the other, she telegraphed her way toward the door.

Where do you think you're going, little one? Do you think I can't see you?

She ignored him. Feeling the edge of the door frame, she groped until the doorknob slipped into her palm. She opened it and stumbled out into the corridor.

A rush of cool air swept over her, enough to make Belial shiver. He lost control and the blackness clouding her vision dissolved. A sob of relief cobwebbed in her chest as she blinked and looked around.

"Beth," she whispered. "I'm coming."

She stumbled down the corridor, limbs shaking with pain and relief. The directional signs were in French and she couldn't read them. At the end of the corridor, she saw two arrows in white, one pointing in either direction. Her options were "Séminaire des Carmes" or "Enregistrement."

She squinted at the word "Séminaire." The accent over the "e" reminded her of the arrow St. George thrust into the dragon's chest. It was just like Belial to bring her to a place where even the alphabet spoke of death.

She looked again at the unfamiliar words.

Seminary, she thought, grasping the corner of the hall-way that turned left.

A whisper of a wing brushed her right frontal lobe. *Very good, little one, this is indeed a seminary. But it was not always so.*

She clung to the wall, moving sideways. If she made it to the street before Belial regained his focus, she could run. She could find a liquor store. Somewhere in her pocket, she had a crumpled bill Beth had given her at the airport. It had been stupid of her not to take any of the bottles of alcohol with her. If she couldn't make it to the street, she had to find someone here who would call Beth to come and get her.

You can't leave, little one. We're not finished yet.

"I changed my mind," she said. At the end of the hallway, she spotted a sign that said "Chapelle." It pointed toward a pair of double doors framed in a pointed gothic arch. She let go of the wall with her right hand and tested her balance. Her knees swayed like a suspension bridge during an earthquake.

I am everywhere. You cannot hide.

"Watch me," Natalie said. She pushed herself off the wall and stumbled through the church's double doors. She staggered past the rows of wooden chairs, and flung herself toward a shadowy side chapel on the right, into a welcoming darkness consumed by shadow and smoke.

CHAPTER SEVEN

Brother *Marius Landry* stepped into the garden and tilted his face to the sky. The late summer sun beat down hotter in Paris than it had in Reims, but he didn't mind. The chapel smelled like a barn, with more than a hundred sweating men in close quarters, but most of them didn't want to go outside. They didn't want to risk being seen by the guards outside the gate. If you were seen, you were abused, either verbally or physically, and they were afraid.

Marius wasn't afraid.

The burning sun was proof that God's order still thwarted the desires of men. The revolutionaries might be able to declare a new constitution and imprison the king, but they could not yet control the weather. They were as sweaty and miserable as their prisoners, and for that, Marius was grateful. He would sit out here and burn, happily, until Père Jean-Honoré called him back inside for their thin supper.

He made his way to a stone bench on the far side of the garden, near the exterior wall. The fruit trees had already been picked clean. Once it turned cold, if they were still imprisoned here, someone would probably cut them down for firewood — their jailors, if they feared giving a prisoner an axe, or one of the prisoners themselves, if the jailors' laziness overcame their fear.

No one had given them any idea how long they would be imprisoned. All over France, deputies descended like flies on a carcass with orders to do this thing or that thing, move someone here or arrest someone there. No one knew who was making the decisions. The king was a prisoner. The pope was too far away to help. Regular people turned their backs on God when crimes occurred.

Just before his arrest and transfer to Paris, a group of townspeople had marched up the hill to the tax collector's house. They tore the door from its hinges, took what they wanted, and smashed the rest. Then they shut the man and his family in the house and set it on fire. When he heard the wife's screams, he'd come up from the schoolhouse and been knocked unconscious by one of the rioters — clapped over the head with a shovel. When he woke up, three houses on the street were smoldering heaps, each with charred piles of flesh and bone inside. They'd given his name to the revolutionary authorities, however, who came to round him up the next morning.

Marius touched the knot on his head and wondered if he ought to be proud. They had only hit him because they thought he might stop them.

It meant they could be stopped.

It meant they could be saved.

But how?

Marius sighed.

Suddenly, he heard the crack of a snapped twig behind him. He spun, half expecting to see the rioter with the shovel again. But it was one of the other prisoners — a slight fellow with large gray eyes and dark hair curling out of his cowl.

He smiled at the young man. "You couldn't bear it in there, either, could you?"

The young man blinked, sending tears down his dirt-streaked cheeks.

Marius reached out a hand. "Is something wrong? Other than the obvious, you know, that we're all in here. If I can do something to help, I will."

The young man turned and fled, running along the garden wall.

Marius shielded his eyes with his hand. As he watched, the young man hurried toward the chapel, ducking behind the stand of fruit trees. "Now where is he going?" Marius muttered. It would be easier to follow the other man's feet than to try and spot him through the leafy trees. But as soon as he ducked down, the feet disappeared. One moment, they were there, at the corner between the north and east walls, and the next … nothing.

Marius blinked.

It wasn't possible.

He rubbed his eyes, got up from his bench, and followed the same path the other man had taken. In the corner, where the young man had disappeared, he stopped. There was no trace of him.

Marius shook his head and wondered if he'd dreamed it. *The sun's not that hot*, he thought.

He crouched and looked at the ground, but it was just ordinary grass. No seam, no trapdoor, no false patch of earth concealing a hidden passage. *Still not possible*, he thought, rising to inspect the stones of the garden wall. *No one could walk through that.* To be sure, he pressed on the stones at chest level. They didn't budge.

"I know what I saw," he said.

As a teacher, a brother of the Frères des Écoles Chrétiennes, it was his job to educate his pupils, to teach them the joy of study and discovery. Admitting intellectual defeat was not something he could stomach. If the boy hadn't been carted off to heaven by a saint or a prophet, he was here … somewhere.

Marius glanced over his shoulder, toward the outer gate facing the Rue de Vaugirard. A woman led a donkey pulling a cart of hay through the street. The guards watched her and whistled.

He turned back to the wall and looked at the masonry. *If I didn't dream it, it happened*, he thought — *the boy went through this wall.* But how? He looked at the way the stones had been laid, the seam of one in the center of the stone above it, layered for strength. Of course it hadn't moved when he pushed it. It couldn't.

Then his eyes drifted to the seam in the corner, where the wall made a ninety-degree turn toward the chapel. It was the only place where the stones lined up evenly. The masons had used stones of different lengths to begin the east wall, but at the point of intersection, by necessity, they all terminated in a straight line.

Marius held his hands at chest level next to the seam.

He pushed.

Nothing happened.

He bent and pushed at a row of stones a hand's length down.

This time, they ground against each other and moved.

A rectangular group of stones, waist high and half as wide, had been mortared together into an iron frame. A rod pierced the frame, anchored in the ground and in the row of stones above it. Pressing on the stones mortared into the frame turned the frame into a swiveling door — swollen and stiff, to be sure, but still movable.

Marius stepped through, ducking his head and pushing the door closed behind him. The frame ground its way back into place, concealing him from the outside world.

He brushed his hands against his black robe and found that they were shaking. *What is this place?* he thought.

The passageway was long and narrow. It appeared to run the length of the chapel, which was on the other side of the left-hand wall. He waited a few moments for his eyes to adjust to the darkness. When he could distinguish shades of gray instead of a uniform curtain of blackness, he crept forward slowly, keeping one hand on the wall. Did the guards know about this tunnel? How had the young man discovered it? In his head, he counted the number of footsteps that carried him away from the door. *Un, deux, trois, quatre, cinq, six ...* by the time he reached *trente-et-un,* the passageway began to curve to the left, around the back of the chapel.

Then he heard it.

A noise, sharper and closer than the muted roar of conversation from the chapel.

He pressed his back to the wall and continued.

Three steps later, he found its source.

The young man sat on the stone floor, back to the wall, knees pulled to his chest. He was crying.

Marius stepped forward. "Don't be frightened," he said, holding both palms up in surrender. "I won't hurt you."

The young man cried out and scrambled backward on all fours. His cowl slipped onto his shoulders and Marius gasped.

"*Calmez-vous*," he said softly, keeping his hands raised. "*Calmez-vous, s'il vous plaît.*"

The frightened young man was actually a frightened young woman. She wore the robe of a Carmelite monk. Thick brown hair curled away from her cheekbones, and dirt streaked her face and forehead.

"I mean you no harm, mademoiselle."

She glared up at him, breathing heavily through her nose. "H — how did you get in here?"

"I followed you."

"Why?"

"You disappeared. I wanted to know where you'd gone."

The girl's wide gray eyes flickered into the darkness over his shoulder.

"I'm alone," he said, exaggerating his movements as he sank to a sitting position on the stone beside her. "No one saw me enter."

"How do I know that?"

"I won't hurt you, I swear." He let a rueful smile tilt his lips. "Bet those deputies would love to hear me say that."

"You were in the garden."

Marius nodded. "Until the guards forbid that, too."

"Will you do it?" she asked. "Swear the oath."

"I don't know."

"They will kill you if you don't. That's what they did to my Reverend Mère."

An inkling of the truth occurred to him and he tilted his head. "Is this your nunnery?"

"Yes."

"Where are the rest of your sisters?"

"Taken away."

"Why did you not go with them?"

"I have a job to do."

"What job?"

She shook her head.

He tried something else instead. "How long have you been in here?"

"Three days."

"Does this passage take you outside, into the street?"

She lifted her shoulders.

"You don't know? That's the first thing I would have tried."

The girl's chin quivered. "I'm scared."

"I'm more scared of being in here," he said. "Aren't you?"

"I've lived behind these walls since I was nine years old. I have nowhere else to go."

"Did your Reverend Mère tell you to hide here?"

"She told me to run."

"So you're disobeying her."

"No," the girl snapped. "I love her."

"I never said you didn't," he soothed. There was something unusual about this girl — a flood of nervous energy that bent the very air around her. He'd had plenty of nervous students before, but this was different. She wasn't a boy, and she wasn't reciting a poem or framing a debate. Her energy was deeper seated, almost frantic. He felt at a loss as to how to help her. "What kind of job are you supposed to do here?" He pointed at her dirty robe. "I can't imagine God would want you to look like one of us to do it."

"I'm h — hiding something."

"Something your Reverend Mère didn't want the deputies to have?"

The girl nodded.

"Can you tell me what it is?"

She shook her head.

"Maybe I could help."

"We're all locked up. No one can help."

"Has anyone tried?"

The girl fixed her wide gray eyes on him and something went through him like a bolt of lightning. He had never felt anything as sharply as the need to calm her, to soothe her, to remove the fear that animated every flash of her eyes.

"Who are you?" he asked.

"I don't know," she said. "But my name is Sister Léonie."

"Is that what you want me to call you?"

"The voice calls me '*little one*.'"

"What voice?"

"The one inside my head."

"I see," he said, although he didn't.

He leaned his head against the wall. What could a nunnery have to hide that was worth risking a girl's life? All over France, he knew monasteries were being seized, along with their contents. Ceremonial vestments and gold plate were being sold, melted, or repurposed to pay for the army. The Prussians were at Longwy, last he'd heard. The Assembly feared that Brunswick would be in Paris within a week.

The girl inched closer to him. "We're all going to die, you know."

"No, I don't know," he replied.

"The voice said so."

"Is the voice God?"

"No."

"Then how do you know? Only God can decide our fate."

"The voice knows God."

"Are you sure?"

"You ask a lot of questions."

"Why don't you? The world is a frightening and amazing place. I'll never stop wondering how and why it works."

"Some things have no answers."

"Everything has an answer."

She looked straight at him. "Why is this happening?"

"Starting with the big questions first, I see."

"You said everything has an answer."

Marius paused. The times he'd turned the question over in his own mind, he'd shied away from the only answer that made sense. Perhaps now, with this girl in his care, he could face it. "They say it's because of the bad harvest and the way the poor pay all the tax while the nobility pays none."

"But you don't believe that."

His fingers picked at a frayed thread in the hem of his robe. "The man who founded my order said we should not expect any reward other than to suffer and die as Jesus Christ did."

"You're a cheerful lot."

"We are teachers, we Brothers of the Christian Schools," he said. "We're accustomed to the resistance of closed minds."

"Then you believe this is happening because one man said you should suffer?"

"No," he said softly, hanging his head. "That's not what I believe."

She slid closer to him, smoothing her robe over her bent knees. "I can't think of anything that would make it right to murder an old woman. Can you?"

He looked sideways at her. "It is bigger than that, I think. Men have grown soft and fat waiting for the second coming of Jesus Christ. There are no more crusades, no more wars of religion, no more English invaders to toss out on their ears."

"You mean their rears," she said. "That's how I would have tossed them."

He smiled at her. "You think you could lift an Englishman? You look too weak to me."

"I could if I had the sword."

"*The* sword? There's more than one, you know. That's part of the problem."

She tucked her chin to her chest and mumbled into the neck of her robe. "Her sword."

"Whose? Your Reverend Mère's?"

The girl shook her head.

"I don't understand."

"I'm afraid," she said, curling her fingers over her knees. "Aren't you?"

"The whole world has caught fire around us." He extended his arm as if he would put it around her, but waited for her to comprehend the gesture. When she leaned into him, he rested his palm on her shoulder gently. "But perhaps I have courage enough for both of us." He bent his head over hers, tucking her against his chest. "It'll be all right."

One small hand reached up to grip his robe, crumpling a handful until her knuckles shone white. "Don't you lie to me."

"*Doucement,*" he said. "I won't lie to you. And I won't let them hurt you."

"Or the s — sword," she whispered.

"Or your sword."

His arms tightened around her and he knew the words were a promise. *We are being tested,* he thought. *And I am going to prove we are worthy.*

CHAPTER EIGHT

Quentin Maillard *slipped* into the room labeled "Rangement" and glanced over his shoulder. The scheduled tour had taken place hours ago. All the smartphone-wielding tourists had long since wandered out through the chapel or the gardens. Still, someone might come to make sure nothing had been stolen or vandalized.

Beneath his black jacket, a shoulder holster held his father's MAC 50 .9mm pistol. His right hand itched to draw it out, though Baptiste had ordered him not to. He would much rather have held the gun than the leather-covered Bible in his right hand.

With a final glance down the hallway, he closed the door behind him.

It was time to get to work.

Before the revolution, this room had belonged to the nunnery's Mother Superior, a woman named Marie-Aimée de Jésus. Baptiste had spent years tracing her genealogy, tracking her movements, and reading her letters. He was sure that anything she had to hide would have been secreted here.

Maillard's own reconnaissance had confirmed Baptiste's hunch. The entire complex of Saint-Joseph-des-Carmes was full of secret doors and passages; the tour guide had pointed one out in the chapel, a secret passage leading away from the pulpit.

Baptiste had told him to look for a door, a place where the mortar between the original limestone blocks wasn't uniform in color, and had sprouted more cracks than the surrounding joints. The more the door was used, the longer and wider the cracks grew.

But as he stepped away from the door, he realized he couldn't look — it was impossible.

Maillard placed his hand against the smooth white wall.

Baptiste hadn't said anything about the original limestone being plastered over.

He had no way of seeing any cracks at all, let alone finding the door.

He ran a finger between the stubble on his neck and the clerical collar of his priest costume. It was too goddamn hot in here, and something about this place made him nervous. He would rather be sent back down the Oyapock River in a pirogue, shooting at gold smugglers, than walking through a seminary pretending to be a priest.

If he couldn't find the door, the entire plan would be delayed by days, if not weeks.

They would need to bring in equipment from Baptiste's university — sonar, radar, and the like. Then they'd have to fabricate a reason for using them.

Maillard stepped toward the room's only window, a single pane of glass overlooking the garden. Beyond the garden lay the sixth arrondissement, home to the Luxembourg Gardens, Les Deux Magots, Café de Flore, and the hotel occupied by the Gestapo during World War II. Paris's streets teemed with life that no force on earth — not the Vikings, not the plague, not the Prussians, and not the Nazis — had been able to extinguish. But now it seemed as if France's own children would do what millennia of invaders could not. They allowed the children of Muslim immigrants to take their jobs, control their streets, change their laws, and alter their customs. At least the English had come under a conqueror's banner. They had never wanted to settle, only to rule.

These new attackers rose from within, yet most Frenchmen did nothing. They seethed behind closed doors, told pollsters they'd vote for Le Pen, but took no real action.

Baptiste was different.

Until he met Baptiste, Maillard had known nothing about Charles Martel, Charlemagne, and the role France had played in saving Europe from Muslim invasion so many centuries before. We are fulfilling the destiny of our ancestors, Baptiste said.

Maillard believed him.

His father would have, too, if he hadn't been blown up by the Armed Islamic Group in 1995. A lieutenant in the Foreign Legion's 1ᵉʳ REP stationed in Algeria in 1961, his father had joined the coup that attempted to overthrow de Gaulle and support the French Algerian settlers who wanted them to stay. But de Gaulle triumphed, and his father was sentenced to a decade in prison. The happiest moment since his father's death was the one in which he and Baptiste had walked into the hospital room of the man who'd left the gas canister on his father's train. The man had been severely burned during the riots in Clichy-sous-Bois, weeks earlier. They had given him muscle relaxers, cut his oxygen supply, and walked out calmly together.

Maillard pulled out the handheld scanner Baptiste had given him. It would only work if the secret door contained material other than limestone or plaster, and if those materials were less than three inches away. It was a long shot, but he owed it to Baptiste to try.

He placed it against the wall. Starting at chest height, he dragged the scanner across the wall from right to left. When he reached the shrine, he stopped.

He'd seen his share of blood, even left quite a bit of his in the Côte d'Ivoire.

This was different.

His head twitched and then his nose. He could have sworn he smelled the ferrous sweetness of fresh blood. His eyes locked onto the blood and traced its path upward, toward the gouges above the rivulets. *A bayonet*, he thought.

Forcing his eyes away, he dropped into a crouch and ran his hands through his hair. On the floor in front of him was a haphazard collection of leaves, fallen from the branch on top of the shrine.

There were three long brown hairs curled on top of the leaves.

Maillard raised his head.

The bustle and vibration of a tour group coming through would surely have shaken a few of those dried leaves loose, but the hair was clearly on top of them.

Someone had been here since the tour group.

Someone who knew about this room and its shrine.

Did they also know what the room concealed?

He jumped to his feet.

Baptiste needed to know, but he couldn't make the call from this room. The noise of his voice might bring someone to investigate. He tugged at his collar and left the room, seeking the blissful cool of the chapel where he could await Baptiste's instructions.

CHAPTER NINE

PRESENT DAY
PARIS, FRANCE

The bathroom was a good thirty yards away from the stage, past a set of double doors everyone would see her burst through on her way out of the auditorium. Beth gulped. *You cannot hurl,* she ordered herself. *You are representing America. Don't be the woman who hurled while representing America.*

She wiped her palms on her black slacks and strode from the back of the room toward the group of men gathered at the front. They stood in a semi-circle around a central figure — a thin man with graying curly hair, a sandy beard, and narrow blue eyes. He wore a blue corduroy blazer and white shirt that probably cost more than her monthly salary. *Fan-fucking-tastic,* she thought. *I'm the only woman on the panel.*

As she approached, the curly-haired man smiled and held out his hand. *"Bonjour,"* he said. "Welcome to the conference.

You must be Elizabeth Brandon." He pronounced "Elizabeth" as *Eh-leez-uh-bet.* "I am Evrard Baptiste."

She reached for his hand and smiled back, hoping there was nothing caught in her teeth. "I know who you are, Dr. Baptiste. I'm honored to be here. Thank you for allowing me to fill in for Dr. Winchester."

"He insisted. And," Baptiste paused, glancing around the circle, "it's obvious the panel needs a woman's perspective. I'm ashamed I didn't invite you first. Please forgive me."

Beth nodded. "Just promise you won't make me answer all the questions about gendered representations of heroism in Frankish texts."

Baptiste laughed. "Mademoiselle Brandon, you have my word."

"Please, call me Beth."

"Beth." His blue eyes settled on her face and she felt vaguely uncomfortable. His stare wasn't the casual once-over of a new acquaintance. It was deep and penetrating, like a film noir detective evaluating a suspect's truthfulness.

"Would you like a glass of wine, Mademoiselle Brandon?" one of the other men asked.

"Yes, please," she said, flashing him a thankful smile.

"I am your host," Baptiste said. "Allow me."

She breathed a sigh of relief as he walked toward a small side table laid out with three bottles and an assortment of hors d'oeuvres. She hadn't felt that uncomfortable under someone's gaze since … *nope*, she thought, smothering a memory of Russia. *Don't even think about it.*

There were still so many unanswered questions about what had happened there.

The things Natalie knew about the Romanov treasure couldn't be explained. Every time she'd asked, Nat would only say that Belial told her. But she didn't believe in ghosts, religion, or the spiritual world. As a single mom juggling a kid, a career, and a mentally ill sister, she didn't have time for an internal debate on the finer points of metaphysical philosophy.

A whisper of fear prickled between her shoulder blades.

This isn't Russia, she told herself. It was a scholarly conference on the formation of the French state and early representations of Frankish kings. So why did the most respected French scholar of the past two decades give her the creeps?

This is ridiculous, she thought, forcing a smile as she accepted a glass of red wine and plate of hors d'oeuvres from Baptiste. "Thank you," she said. "Is this a Bordeaux? I saw a viticulture professor use the hashtag #yoleaux the other day and I was jealous."

"France has many treasures, Mademoiselle Brandon. Wine is only one of them."

Treasure.

Another word she didn't want to hear. She held the glass to her lips and took a sip.

"Do you like it?" Baptiste asked. His lips were cracked in a half-smile that was poised to explode in full or fall like a shooting star. "I'd be happy to send the last bottle back for you to share with your..."

"Sister," she said. "I came with my sister."

"Will she be joining you at the presentation tomorrow?"

Beth shook her head. "Nat hates crowds. Besides, she wasn't feeling well when I left the hotel. In fact, if you'll excuse me, I want to check on her." She held onto her wine and hors d'oeuvres with one hand and reached for her phone with the other. She turned away from the group and hurried toward the back of the room.

Why wouldn't the shiver between her shoulder blades go away? She had an opportunity most scholars would kill for, and she was ruining it because her host made her feel … icky.

It sounded stupid, even to her.

"Get a grip," she mumbled. "You're fine, Nat's fine, and there's a bottle of free wine calling your name."

She looked down at her phone, finger paused over the hotel's number, saved in her contacts just in case. Instead of calling, she swiped back to the phone's home screen and accessed a collection of documents in her cloud storage—Natalie's medical records. As her sister's legal guardian, she never went anywhere without access to these files. Mostly because she knew that if anything ever happened to Nat, she'd be too much of a wreck to explain. Hell, she couldn't explain now.

She imagined a foreign doctor looking at the scanned documents for the first time:

Patient's temporary coma remains unexplained. MRI reveals overdeveloped hypothalamus with extraordinary power of suggestion—possible cause of the somatic delusion described. Upon emergence, patient reports consistent auditory and visual hallucinations, all referencing an angel named Belial. Referring patient to children's psychiatric ward for further evaluation.

—Dr. Edward Hinman, St. Mary's Medical Center, 1993

Patient displays signs of recurrent psychosis with certain long-term deterioration in functional capacity. Reports frequent auditory hallucinations. Administered immediate dosage of Thorazine; recommended long-term treatment plan with continued use of antipsychotics and mood stabilizers.
   —Dr. Thomas Gridley, SF General Hospital, 1997

Patient exhibits anhedonia, avolition, affective flattening and dysphoric mood, characteristic of moderate to severe schizophrenia. According to family member (sister), symptoms worsened with Prolixin.
   —Dr. Samantha Thompson, Cal Pacific Medical Center, 1998

Patient is unresponsive and uncommunicative. Persistent auditory hallucinations severely affect patient's communication and judgment. GAF score: 32 out of 100. Recommended institutionalization, but guardian (sister) refused.
   —Dr. Emil Berg, SF Community Health Network, 2002

Patient admitted after suicide attempt. Claims a characterized auditory hallucination, an angel named Belial, told her to do it. Despite persistent auditory hallucinations, patient displays advanced metabolic function in frontal cortex. Performs exceedingly well in higher thought process tests, including abstraction and concept formation.
   —Dr. Jabez Harger, St. Luke's Hospital, 2007

She hesitated again, ready to swipe back to her contact list and call the hotel.

"Mademoiselle Brandon?" Baptiste called. "Is everything all right?"

The rest of the men stopped talking. She heard the rustle of fabric as they all turned to look at her. If she didn't know better, she'd have thought Baptiste did it on purpose. *Dickweed*, she thought. *Do not give him the satisfaction of freaking out.*

Beth slid her finger off the home screen.

Natalie was fine. She had to be.

She downed the rest of the wine and tossed the phone back into her bag. "Couldn't be better," she said, turning on her heel and grinning as if her life depended on it.

CHAPTER TEN

PRESENT DAY
PARIS, FRANCE

The tomb-like chill of the tile crept into her bones. Natalie smiled. Belial hated the cold. Like a hibernating creature in a state of suspended animation, the chill made him slow his breathing, his thoughts, his movements, his everything. It wasn't as effective as alcohol, but it was a lot less dangerous. She pressed her fingertips into the floor, remembering something a shrink had told her about the hands being a center of healing energy.

The chapel's ceiling arched in painted glory above her. The Virgin Mary held out her hands in supplication as a handsome shirtless man — her son? — held a crown over her head. Natalie's gaze drifted down the blue-and-gold stained-glass window to the decorative gold columns beneath it. It was one of the most beautiful places she'd ever seen.

"Mademoiselle?"

The voice came from everywhere and nowhere, echoing between the marble floor and ceiling.

Shit, she thought. *It's the voice of God. He's speaking to me now, too.* The thought made her want to dissolve her bones and seep into the cracks of the floor, down into the belly of the earth where it was warm and dark and no angels could find her.

"Mademoiselle?"

"Go away," she said, covering her face with her hands. If she counted every speck of dust on the floor, maybe God would lose interest in her. Maybe he'd be polite enough to wait for her to finish before talking to her again. She'd split the dust particles with the tips of her fingernails until they became infinite. That way, neither God nor his angels could ever speak to her again.

A priest in a black suit crouched beside her. Strong hands grasped her arms, pulling her into a sitting position. "Mademoiselle," he said. "*Vous êtes blessée?*"

The silver buttons on his shirt glowed in the chapel's dim light. His white collar circled his neck like a noose. "Are you hurt?" he asked, this time in heavily accented English.

The man had thick blond hair, and a nose that hooked and planed in a shape she'd only seen on ancient coins. Hands still under her arms, he glanced behind them, toward the exit. "The church is closed for the evening, mademoiselle."

"I'm not hurt," she said. "I just needed a place to hide."

Lashes longer than hers brushed his olive cheekbones. "From whom?"

"Belial. He brought me to see the shrine."

He forced a tight smile. "You are here with someone, then?"

"I'm alone."

"Did your friend already leave?"

"He never leaves, even when I ask him to."

"Mademoiselle, are you sure you're not ill?"

Of course you are not ill, Belial grumbled. *Why is that always their first question?*

"Pretty sure," she said. "An illness goes away."

Footsteps shuffled past the other side of the chapel's doors, and the priest's shoulders twitched. A faint body odor wafted from the folds of his clothing as he moved. "You cannot be here now, mademoiselle."

She pointed at his white collar. "Do you believe in angels?"

He blinked. "I'm a priest. I believe everything the Bible says."

"You shouldn't."

The priest's amber eyes narrowed. "Why not?"

"It says that angels minister to the heirs of salvation, but it isn't true. They minister to themselves. If it's wrong about that, there's no telling what else it's wrong about."

Is that what you think of me, little one?

"You don't want to know," she said, addressing the air in front of her. Her head pounded, her body ached, and the sweat drying on her skin felt like it was shrinking her.

"Will I have to escort you out of the building, mademoiselle?" Fading daylight from the stained-glass window flickered against his hair. "Public visiting hours are over."

"It's God's house, not yours."

"We have classes," he said, through clenched teeth. "You are not enrolled in the institute."

"Belial was going to show me something."

"How did your … friend … know about the shrine?"

She looked at the priest's loose black shirt and pants. Suddenly, it made sense that both priests and doctors wore clothing that looked like pajamas. They fumbled with souls and bones the way sleepwalkers fumbled with the doorknobs that kept them in their bedrooms at night. "You tell me. I don't think he feels like talking right now."

On the contrary, Belial replied. *Ask him if he wants to know his father's last words.*

"No."

Do it, Belial ordered, lashing her with a wing.

She cried out and fell forward. The priest had no choice but to catch her against his chest. She craned her neck to look up at him, but there was no warmth in his solid amber gaze. His face was hard, carved in right angles out of granite. "B — Belial says he knows what your father's last words were."

The priest gripped her arms until she cried out.

"You're hurting me," she said.

He is thinking of doing more than that.

"You should not have said that, mademoiselle," the priest growled.

Tell him his father's last thoughts were of Algeria. Of the coup. Of the help promised by Bissell and Dulles that never came.

"What?" Natalie moaned. "He won't believe me. I don't even believe you."

That's why it's called faith.

She clamped her lips shut. Before Belial, she had been like any other girl, with faith in rainbows and crayons and sharpened pencils. It had spared her nothing. Neither God nor Allah nor Buddha had saved her.

You still don't understand, little one. I'm the one who saved you from them.

"Angels are such shitty liars."

The priest moved his hands from her upper arms to her face, pressing painfully in a parody of a lover's caress. "I hope for your sake, mademoiselle, they are not."

CHAPTER ELEVEN

AUGUST 18, 1792
PARIS, FRANCE

arius slipped into the passageway through the secret door in the garden. Most of the other prisoners in the chapel had fallen into trancelike prayer, swaying on their knees in near darkness. The rest slept anywhere they could find a place to lay their heads. No one had said a word when he tossed, turned, sighed, and got up.

He pushed on the secret door to swing it shut behind him. He was sure no one had seen him. The guards left them alone at night, maintaining a presence only at the outer gate. They wanted no part of a crowded room filled with more than a hundred unwashed men.

Night, for almost a week now, had brought no relief from the heat. The stench of sweat and fear hung heavy over all of Paris.

The iron frame of the secret door scraped against the stone above it as he ground it into place. He winced, hoping no one in the chapel would come to investigate. He pressed his hands to the stone and waited. When no voices or footsteps sounded on the other side of the door, he breathed a sigh of relief.

The sigh didn't slow the fierce pounding of his heart.

It had been one full day since he'd first seen Léonie and he could think of nothing else.

The moment when she'd grasped his robe and pressed her face to his chest had set something loose in him. He wanted to protect her, to try to make whole what the Assembly and the revolutionaries were destroying. If she were the challenge God had set before him, he accepted gladly.

He exhaled slowly as he walked the length of the passage, rounding the corner that led past the altar and the choir. *You will see a stone staircase*, Léonie had said. *Climb it and it will lead you to me.*

Marius climbed slowly, one hand on the wall as he waited for his eyes to adjust. His fingers brushed over empty sconces and he shuddered, imagining they were thin devils' arms reaching for him as he passed. The stone steps were taller than he was used to, and he felt his breath shorten as he neared the top.

When he ascended the final stair, a narrow passage-way appeared before him. Suddenly, Léonie appeared from a patch of darkness on the right. "In here," she said, pulling him into a stone chamber that had no door and no windows. In the absence of light, all he could see was the glow of her face.

"Where are we?" he asked, looking around the room as if there were anything to see but darkness.

"This room connects to a cell in the nunnery."

He resisted the urge to touch her face. "Are you all right? You haven't let anyone see you?"

"Of course not."

"Look." He pushed up the sleeve of his black robe. "I brought you something."

Earlier that night, he'd stolen a burlap sack from the makeshift scullery, torn it in half with his teeth, and piled each square with a crust of bread and an apple. Then he secured the tops with a skein of burlap and tied the ends around his upper arms like tourniquets. The robe's voluminous sleeves hid his crime from the other men.

"You stole from them," Léonie said.

"Only to feed you." Marius smiled. "Surely that's a transgression you can overlook?"

Léonie's stomach rumbled. "Hmph," she said, reaching for the knots in the burlap ties.

She slid her nails between the skeins of a knot and tried to force them apart. As she worked, her knuckles brushed the skin of his inner arm. Marius bit his lip. He wasn't used to being touched. He knew, of course, what it was like to lie with a woman. He hadn't taken his vows until the age of twenty-two. It had been years, though, and not something he had expected to miss. But now, Léonie's unintentional touch unleashed a flood of thoughts no priest should have.

Léonie growled deep in her throat. "These knots are too tight. You should have brought me a knife."

Marius bit back his reply: *Then I wouldn't have felt your hands on my skin.*

It was a sin to think it, but he thought it.

It was a sin to feel it, but he felt it.

He closed his eyes and tried to contain his thoughts.

"Maybe I should use my teeth," she said, leaning toward him.

"No!" he said, pulling his arm away.

Léonie blinked. "Did I do something wrong?"

"Of course not. I'm sorry. I didn't mean to snap at you."

"I wasn't going to bite your arm." She motioned for him to come toward her once more. "Why would you think that?"

He held out his right arm again. This time, she picked up the bottom of one of the burlap sacks and held it to her mouth. Her teeth tore through the thin weave easily, dropping a crust of bread and an apple into her waiting hand. "There, you see?"

Without the pressure of its contents, the string tourniquet loosened on his arm. This time, she was able to untie the knot without difficulty. "There," she said, sliding a gentle finger across the red welt left by the burlap tie. "Did that hurt?"

He let out a shaky breath and tried to tamp down the flame of heat licking at his belly. "It will," he said softly.

"Give me the other."

Marius pushed up his left sleeve. She repeated the process so quickly this time that he barely felt the whisper of her touch. "You're a quick study."

"I'm so hungry." She dropped to her knees and began a prayer of thanksgiving for the food. She crossed herself before reaching for an apple. "Was this dangerous for you?"

"No," he lied.

"Thank you."

"You're welcome."

"I could go out and eat with them, you know," she said, sinking her teeth into the apple. "Then you wouldn't have to —"

"Don't," he said, grabbing her arm as forcefully as he dared. "One look and they'd know you aren't one of them. If the guards found out…" He remembered what the men with pikes and torches had said to the tax collector's wife. Perhaps it was best that they'd bashed him on the head. If they had done what they said they were going to do, they'd have had to kill him first. "You don't know what they're like."

"I know exactly what they're like," she snapped. "I watched them kill the Reverend Mère."

"She was an old woman. It would be different with you, I think."

Léonie licked a drop of apple juice that had fallen onto her chin. "They'd rape me, you mean."

"Yes, that's what I mean."

"I'm not a child. You can say it."

"How old are you?"

She narrowed her gray eyes at him. "How old are *you*?"

"Twenty-six," he answered.

"Nineteen," she replied. For a moment, her face went blank and then she frowned and shook her head.

"What was that?" he asked.

"The voice said something beastly."

"He doesn't like me?"

"He said you won't see twenty-seven."

Marius felt a tingle of fear between his shoulders. He had been twenty-six for eleven months. "Let's hope he's wrong."

Léonie looked away. "I've been thinking about what you said. About this happening because there are no more crusades to test the strength of our devotion to God."

He studied the line of her profile — prominent cheekbones, sharp chin, straight nose. Her face was too angular to be beautiful the way the queen was said to be beautiful. But he found Léonie a thousand times more affecting than the portraits of the vacant-eyed round-faced queen. "I'm not sure what I think anymore," he said.

"But you're right. It fits the pattern."

"What pattern?"

"Acre, the last crusader stronghold, fell 501 years ago. Actually, it fell 501 years, three months, and twelve days ago, to be exact."

He shook his head. "I don't understand."

"In the Bible, there are approximately five hundred years between Abraham and the Exodus, between the Exodus and King David, between David and Daniel, between Daniel and the birth of Jesus Christ. If it's been five hundred years since our last test, we're more than due."

"Léonie, how on earth did you count that out?"

She looked away, as if she were ashamed of the answer. "In my head. I see the sums, written as clearly as if they were on paper."

"And the exact date that Acre fell?"

"The Reverend Mère taught us about the crusades the second year I was here."

"How long ago was that?"

"Ten years."

"And you remembered it all this time?"

"I don't have a heart, so there's room inside me for other things."

He smiled, but only until he realized Léonie wasn't smiling back. "That's not true, you know."

"It is," she said, nodding. "Everyone in my village knew. It's why my parents brought me here. Well, the heart and the voice."

"God would never create a woman without a heart."

"But He did." Léonie sank to the floor and leaned her cheek against the wall. "I didn't cry," she said softly. "My brother died and I laughed as my father lowered his body into the ground."

"Why did you laugh?"

"The voice told me a riddle. He said he wanted to ease my pain."

"Did you tell your parents that's why you laughed?"

She nodded. Her fingers fell to the hem of her robe and she picked at it with her nails. "They said I shouldn't have listened. Or that I should have been so sad nothing could overcome my grief."

"How old was your brother?"

"Twelve days."

"You barely knew him."

"He was my brother and I laughed at his corpse. The whole village saw me do it."

"Children do odd things," he said. "I don't understand why the littlest ones want to eat dirt and put everything in their mouths, but I know it doesn't mean anything sinister."

"My mother could not forgive me." Léonie blinked and two tears fell down her cheeks. "They brought me here not long afterward."

"Because you laughed?"

"Because I'm me. Because the voice talks to me and they were afraid it's a demon."

"It's not a demon."

"You don't know that."

He sank to his knees beside her. One hand reached out to touch her cheek. "There's no demon in you, Léonie."

"Then what is it?" she whispered, raising her hand to his, keeping it pressed to her face. "What is this thing inside me that can speak but never appear?"

"I don't know," he said.

"Why do people hate me because of it?" Her chin quivered. "I was just a child. Why did God want the world to hate a child? Am I some hideous thing, born while His back was turned?"

Marius did the only thing he could think of to do. He brought both hands to the sides of her face and leaned forward. He rested his lips against hers, calm and soft. It was simple and elemental, merely the warmth and comfort of another human being caught up in the same conflagration. If God had truly turned His back on them, He would never know what they did in His absence.

When he pulled back, he wiped the tears from her cheeks. "You must never think that."

"What am I, then, if not a monster?"

"A beautiful soul," he said, "trapped in a terrible cage."

Léonie pulled away, but not before he saw her bite her lip to hold back a smile. "Come," she said. "I want to show you something."

CHAPTER TWELVE

The fog was moving, she was sure of it. Natalie chose one bulbous fold of gray and followed it with her eyes as it swirled past the corner of the house. Even though individual ripples and folds moved, there was never an end. The fog went on forever, blocking the sun and sky in every direction. It didn't make sense. Only the sky was as big as the sky.

"You should have brought a jacket," Beth said, pointing at the goosebumps on her arms.

"I don't want one." It didn't seem right to worry about the cold when she was here to bury her second-best friend. The white jewelry box on the ground near Beth held the remains of Medusa, her pet tarantula. She'd died sometime while Natalie was in the hospital. Beth said their father had been the one to pull the body out of the terrarium and place it in the box.

"Are you ready?" Beth said, picking up the shovel.

No, Natalie thought. *I'll never be ready.*

Her terrarium had sat on a round table next to her bed. It had a small light, so she could turn it on and watch Medusa anytime she wanted, even at night. Most people thought spiders were gross, but that's why she loved them. People forgot they were fast and smart and helpful because they ate other bugs. All you had to do was leave them alone and they would help you, or at least not bother you. But people couldn't do that. They had to squish them and kill them without giving them a chance.

Just like me, Natalie thought.

She looked down at the patch of gauze and tape on her arm. The big needle the nurse had put in her hurt when it came out. It had made weird things tingle between her skin and her bones. She still didn't understand why they'd done it or what had happened to her. One minute she'd been standing at the chalkboard in Mrs. Norton's class. The next, she'd felt something move beneath her skull—a creature with human form and feather-covered wings. It tried to open its wings, but the pressure hurt so much it blacked out her vision. When the thing realized her skull was the obstacle, it raised its head and spoke to her from behind her own face. "I have things I need to show you, but I have to open my wings to do it. Will you let me?"

There was no way she could have stopped it, so she agreed. Her body fell to the floor. Suddenly, she could see her body as she and the creature floated side by side above it. "My name is Belial," it said, using a man's voice. "I live inside you now."

"Are you an angel?"

But he wouldn't answer. He just took her to a place where strange gray snow fell from the sky. A chimney spewed black smoke and men trudged past her wearing their pajamas. They were tired and they asked to stop, but another man in black whipped them until they moved again. One of them fell down and the man in black whipped him until the pajamas fell away and something red came out of his mouth. Then the man in black turned around and looked straight at her. She screamed in terror and woke up in a hospital bed, choking on the taste of flesh and ashes.

The doctors couldn't explain it. They told her parents that her heart rate had fallen to twenty-nine beats per minute, resulting in a coma. They didn't say anything about Belial.

True to his word, the angel had taken up residence in her head. He perched in the space between her brain tissue and her skull. It hurt when he moved and every time he shifted his wings, the tips of his feathers pricked her brain, like thousands of tiny needles. When she tried to explain this to the doctor, he shook his head and said it was impossible. She told him to look for Belial on an X-ray, but he found the wrong thing — all he wanted to talk about was something called the limbic system. He said she was autistic, but the other doctor he brought in said she was schizophrenic, a rare early-onset case. The only thing they agreed on was that she should be pumped full of olanzapine until she couldn't think of anything to say at all.

The next few days had been a blur of lights, electric shocks, and big pills that made her choke when she tried to swallow them. Ever since she'd started swallowing them, she said things that were stupid and thought things that were even stupider. People used to tell her mother how smart she was — after reading a poem, she could recite it. After hearing someone say something, she remembered it. But something in the medicine was making her forget how to be smart.

Her mother didn't care.

She brought a new tray of pills every morning and watched Natalie while she put them in her mouth. She checked under Natalie's tongue and in the folds of her cheeks to make sure she swallowed them, and wouldn't let her go to her room for an hour afterward in case she tried to throw them up.

It was too hard to fight, and much easier to do what they all wanted.

So that's what she did … or tried to do, at least.

The thing that said it was an angel talked to her more now, too. It told her what had happened to Medusa as soon as she'd stepped out of the car on the way home from the hospital. She'd run inside, looking for her terrarium, but it was already gone. The thing told her what her mother was making for dinner, what time her father would get home from work, and when someone was lying to her. This, at least, was useful.

Look behind you, little one, the voice said.

Natalie looked over her shoulder to the kitchen window. Her mother dropped the curtain and quickly moved away.

Someday, I'll tell you who you are and where you come from — a long line of women who were stronger than they knew.

Natalie looked at Beth's hands, clutching the shovel that dug into the earth. Her sister's knuckles glowed white as she moved shovelful after shovelful of earth. "I know that," she said.

Finally, when the hole was deep enough, Beth set the shovel down. Natalie's chin quivered as Beth picked up the white box. "Do you want to do the honors?" her sister asked.

She didn't know. Part of her wanted to hold the box to her chest, hugging it the way she couldn't hug her pet in real life. But if she touched the box, she knew she'd open the lid — and that couldn't happen. Spiders curled up when they died, and that wasn't the way she wanted to remember Medusa. But on the other hand, saying no meant that Beth had to do it, and this wasn't Beth's job.

Natalie held out her hands.

Gently, her sister placed the white box in her grasp. "Goodbye, Medusa," she said, stroking the lid of the box. She crouched down and placed the box in the hole. "I miss you."

She stood up and felt her eyes burn with tears. Everything would be different now. Her room was empty, without another living creature in it. She wouldn't hear the scrabble of Medusa's thick legs against the moss and bark in the terrarium. She wouldn't put her palm against the glass and see Medusa raise one furry leg in greeting.

Cheer up, little one, the voice said.

"I don't want to cheer up."

"You don't have to," Beth said. "It's okay to be sad."

Natalie bit her lip. She'd done it again — forgotten to answer the voice in silence.

Beth hoisted the shovel and used her foot to push it into the earth. "Are you ready?" she asked, before lifting the shovelful of dirt.

No, Natalie thought, feeling a tear slip down her cheek. *I want my friend back. She'll be cold and lonely out here in the backyard.*

Hush, the voice said. *I'll be your friend now.*

I want Medusa, Natalie thought. *Not you.*

She nodded at Beth to give her the go-ahead. Her sister tipped the shovel over the white box, using the flat head to smooth the rough clumps of dirt into a sort of blanket. Beth always knew the right thing to do, the right thing to say.

"She'll be warm now," Natalie said. "T—thank you, Beth."

I know how to cheer you up. I'll tell you a joke—it's a tradition.

Don't laugh, Natalie ordered herself. *It isn't right. You have to be sad right now.*

I heard that, the voice said. *I'm a part of you, remember? But you're grieving, so I won't take it personally. Now, listen…there once was a man suffering from a terrible illness. A friar came to comfort him. The friar told him to be of good cheer because God chastens those He loves most. "Ah," said the sick man. "No wonder He has so few friends."*

The laugh started somewhere behind her eyes. It made them crinkle, like when she smiled or squinted at the sun. Then it tumbled out through her mouth before she could stop it.

You see? the voice said. *I only want to help you.*

"Nat," Beth said. "Are you okay?"

Natalie put her hands over her face and sank to the ground. Her sister set the shovel down and knelt beside her. "Come here," Beth said, opening her arms.

Natalie tumbled into them, sobbing.

"Cry all you want," Beth said, stroking her hair. "Just let it all out."

Let it all out. Did that mean if she cried hard enough, the creature inside her would go back where it came from?

It doesn't work that way, little one, it said. *And I do have a name.*

Beth pressed her lips to Natalie's forehead. "I wish I could tell you things get easier, kiddo. But I don't think they do."

"It'll be okay," Natalie said. "As long as we have each other."

Beth squeezed her tight. "You are the goddamn bravest kid I know."

Natalie smiled. "You said a bad word."

"You won't tell on me, will you?"

"Never."

An ocean-borne breeze blew droplets of fog into their faces. "You sure you're not cold?" Beth asked.

"Maybe a little."

"Let's finish up, then," Beth said, getting up to retrieve the shovel. She piled more heaps of dirt over the white box until it was invisible. Then she smoothed the dirt over again, and planted the popsicle-stick cross Natalie had made, tied together with purple ribbon. When Beth finished, she stood next to her and reached for her hand.

For a moment, she felt safe — not happy, but safe.

You are not alone, little one. There were others like you.

She thought about the curtains moving in the kitchen window. *Is my mom one?* she asked silently.

You are all my girls. It is her bloodline that calls to me.

She said nothing.

I only want to help you. Keep you safe.

"From what?"

If you knew what was coming, you would not wish me away.

The droplets of mist pelting her face were like miniature tears. She looked into the cold gray nothingness above her, wondering who was above the clouds, crying. Before the hospital, she'd been afraid of jumping off the jungle gym, or of feeling the sharp sting of antiseptic spray on a skinned knee. Now she knew how small those fears were. The monsters and creatures she read about in books weren't made up at all. They were alive, inside people. She wondered if they all claimed to be angels, tricking people into doing what they wanted.

You will never control me, Natalie thought. *Do you hear me? I hear you,* the voice said. *I just don't believe you.*

CHAPTER THIRTEEN

vrard Baptiste smiled at the communist professor from Lyon and tilted his plate of hors d'oeuvres to glance at his smartwatch. Maillard should have checked in by now with the agreed-upon code: Orléans for success and Agincourt for failure. How long could it possibly take to run a handheld scanner over four walls?

Unless someone had interrupted him.

Unless he'd been caught.

Baptiste's smile turned to a grimace. He'd selected Maillard for this job specifically because of his background. The younger man had spent his first nineteen years believing he was bound for the priesthood. He had the knowledge and vocabulary to fool most onlookers into thinking he belonged in Saint-Joseph-des-Carmes. He also had the military training to incapacitate anyone who tried to keep him from his goal. What the hell was taking him so long?

He glanced at his watch again.

"I'm sorry," Yves Collant said, tilting his head. "Am I boring you?"

Yes, Baptiste thought. *You're a communist. You've been wrong for a hundred years and you're wrong today.* "Of course not," he said, tilting his plate. "I thought I was about to spill onto the carpet."

The American woman's eyes dropped to his plate and registered the fact that his baked brie was nowhere near the edge of the plate. She looked back at him with a curious stare.

"Mademoiselle Brandon," he said smoothly. "I'd love to hear your thoughts on the matter."

"Cheese? I'm all for it."

Irritation surged and he raised his voice. "Don't you agree that the results achieved by the National Assembly during the revolution are impossible to duplicate today because of our country's fractured racial identity?"

"I don't know," she said, picking up a tarte flambée. "Why don't you ask Alexandre Dumas, père?"

"The son of a marquis."

"The son of a slave," she shot back.

"One drop in a flood, Mademoiselle Brandon. But today, there are more than five million such drops. They want to bring religion into our schools, into public office. They will not work, yet they want all the benefits of a tax-supported state. Is this progress?"

The woman had the decency to blush. "Americans aren't the best people to ask about race. Or haven't you heard Billie Holiday sing 'Strange Fruit'?"

"But I am asking you," he said, taking a sip of wine. The tannins left a bitter taste in his mouth and he grimaced. "Our National Assembly legislated things that people believed it was impossible to legislate. The election of clergy, for example. Would it not be better to put religion in the hands of an organized body who can guide its citizens to better choices?"

"Guide?" the woman said. "Or force? With all due respect, Dr. Baptiste, this is a slippery slope that, once upon a time, could have led to this conversation being conducted in German."

"A nation cannot survive without a unified culture. That is its soul. How else can it preserve the treasures that teach us who and what we are? The monuments that show us what we've achieved? The common language that connects us with our heroes and martyrs?" He leaned toward her. "When people forget their nation has a soul, it leads them to do terrible things. Of all those here, you should understand that."

The red flush spread from the American woman's cheeks to her throat. She glanced from side to side, looking for help. The communist, Yves Collant, stared at his shoes.

But the man on her right, Malone Marchand, gave her a nod.

Baptiste glared at him.

Marchand, a Sorbonne professor specializing in armed conflict and international relations from the fourth through tenth centuries, had rejected every overture he'd made over the past few years. It was inconceivable that someone who had studied the Battle of Tours and the Moorish conquest of

Spain could fail to see the danger in the current flood of Arab immigrants and refugees. The man was myopic at best, blind at worst — with terrible taste in women. His eyes hadn't left the American woman's face since she'd entered the room.

"I'm sorry," the woman said. "I thought we here to talk about French history. I only debate American politics in my other shoes."

"What other shoes?" asked Malone Marchand.

"Steel-toed boots," she replied, her blue gaze focused squarely on him.

You are a coward, he wanted to say. Instead, he flung out his hand at the conference banner hung behind the stage. "Only the small-minded separate history and politics, Mademoiselle Brandon. Perhaps I made a mistake in inviting you."

"I teach history," she said. "I want my students to make up their own minds about politics."

"They are one and the same! Look around you, mademoiselle. We are the few who understand this nation's soul. We cherish it, we keep alive the memory of Charles Martel and Charlemagne and Jeanne d'Arc. We know how our nation responds to threats — we have seen it demonstrated in the writings of the past! And since we are the ones who understand it best, we are responsible for making sure this nation lives up to its destiny, now, in our lifetime!" He waited for the echoes of his voice to fade. "Or did you think this was just a free vacation?"

The American woman glared at him over the rim of her glass.

He smiled, pleased to see her speechless. Perhaps his words had finally made an impression on her.

"We all understand that we're here to explore and celebrate our country's history," said Malone Marchand. "There's no need to frighten Dr. Brandon."

"I'm not scared," the woman said.

"You will see," he said, narrowing his eyes at Marchand. "You'll all see! This nation will be great again. All she needs is a guardian, a caretaker — a shepherd to keep the wolves at bay."

This time, the American woman smiled.

"What?" he snapped.

"I don't trust shepherds."

"Why not?"

"That thing they lean on? It's called a crook."

Baptiste growled and looked at his watch. *Americans,* he thought. *Sometimes no better than the infidel.*

CHAPTER FOURTEEN

"*Let go of* me," Natalie said.

The priest's palms were hot against her cheeks. His breath swayed the loose strands of her long, tangled hair. "You don't know anything about my father."

"Algeria," she whispered.

His hands fell from her face.

She scrambled backward, out of his grasp.

They remained on the floor, panting and staring at each other in the dim light from the stained-glass window.

"Who are you?" he said.

"I could ask you the same thing." She felt his amber gaze bore into her, searching for something that would explain how she'd known. She gazed back, looking for evidence that he was one of God's chosen. He didn't look like any priest she'd ever met. His skin was tan, the color set deeply into the lines on his forehead. She glanced at his hands. They were the same color. "I thought being a priest was an indoor thing."

"Sometimes my work takes me to places I would rather not go."

Ask him what work he does, Belial said. *Let him lie to you here in the house of the Lord.*

"Belial wants to know what work you do."

"I do the work my superior sets before me."

"Sounds like a waste of free will."

"Order must be preserved, mademoiselle."

"Whose blood is in that shrine upstairs?"

"I don't know."

"Why doesn't Belial like you?"

"I don't know."

"He brought me here for a reason, and I'm not leaving until I find out what it is. You can help me, or you can throw me out, but I'm just going to come back. I made him a promise. I have to keep it."

He crouched in a squat, as if warming himself at a campfire. "How did you know about Algeria?"

"Tell me about that shrine, and I'll tell you what Belial said."

"An exchange," he said. "Words instead of hostages."

"You go first, or I'll scream and tell someone you grabbed me."

He paused, glancing over her shoulder toward the nave. "I can only tell you what I have been told." When she nodded, he continued. "During the revolution, this church was turned into a prison. The men held here were priests who refused to swear allegiance to the government in place of the pope."

"Refractory priests," she said. A sinking feeling in her stomach told her where the story would end, but she let him speak.

"There were more than a hundred here who refused to take the oath. There was supposed to be a trial, but it was September."

She blinked and a vision of smoke and gunpowder and blood appeared before her eyes. "The massacres," she whispered.

Belial lowered his head in a posture of grief. *Liberty, Liberty, what have they done to thee? What horrors are committed in thy name!*

She'd first read about the September massacres as a kid. The Parisian mob had emptied the city's prisons and butchered the inhabitants. They feared the prisoners would escape and join the advancing Prussian army, or that the Prussians would take Paris and enlist the prisoners anyway. To keep either option from happening, they killed them all — men, women, nuns, priests, old, young, guilty, innocent.

"The priests died here?" she asked, pulling her legs to her chest.

"Not in this chapel, if that's what you were thinking."

The scar on her left arm began to itch. She pushed up her sleeve to scratch it.

He followed her movement, tracing the long, thin scar with his eyes. "You are brave," he said.

"Technically, I'm a failure."

"Most people ..." He made a slashing gesture across his wrists. "Not as effective."

Belial smiled. *What God has joined together, let no man put asunder.*

"That's a weird thing for a priest to know," she said.

"I was not always a priest."

"What were you?"

"A soldier."

"Got tired of killing people?"

"They wouldn't let me kill the right ones."

"Who are the right ones?"

"The people who killed my father," he said softly. "He was betrayed by his commanding officers. And then by his country."

"But you gave all that up," she said, pointing to his collar.

Did he, little one?

Natalie shivered. She closed her eyes and lightning forked behind her lids, in the same downward spread as the rivulets of blood in the shrine. "I want to go home," she said. "I want Beth."

The priest grabbed her arm. "Tell me what else you know about my father."

She took a breath, prepared to tell him she didn't know a damn thing, when the same female voice she'd heard outside the church echoed inside her skull. The words were soft, feathery, mirrored: *When I was thirteen, I had a voice from God to help me govern myself. The first time, I was terrified.*

"But I was nine," she moaned, feeling tears fill her eyes.

Then I suppose that isn't you, is it, little one?

"Who is it?" she cried.

I'm ashamed you would even have to ask.

"Thirteen," she said. "A voice from God."

"What was that?" The priest grabbed her other arm and shook her. "What did you say?"

"Joan," she whispered. "It's Joan, isn't it?"

Joan of Arc's voices had come to her in the fields of Domrémy, in eastern France, when she was thirteen. The Archangel Michael had come to her first, she'd said, followed by Saint Catherine and Saint Margaret. But what did Joan have to do with Belial, or this church, or the blood shrine? Joan was long dead by the time the French Revolution began. It wasn't her blood on that limestone wall.

"Who told you?" the priest snapped. "Who told you it was here?"

His grip held fast when she tried to shake free.

She looked down at his right hand, clutching her forearm. At the base of his index finger, just above the knuckle, a pale stripe of flesh matched the color of her white T-shirt.

A ring, she thought. *What sort of priest wears a thick band on his index finger?*

Something in her stomach began to churn. The chapel's air felt leaden in her lungs, weighted with dust motes flecked from stones older than her country.

She looked at the priest, dressed all in black except for the slim white noose circling his neck. "You're not a priest," she said. "Are you?"

The man lunged for her.

As he moved, she saw a thin green tattoo around his neck, beneath the white collar of his costume. He grabbed her hair and she kicked as hard as she could. He fell backward, pulling out a hank of her hair.

She scrambled to her feet and dashed into the nave.

He was still clutching her hair when he got up. "It was you," he said. "You were at the shrine. You can't have it. It belongs to us!"

"I don't even know what you're talking about!"

The man threw down her hair and stalked toward her. Natalie dashed down an aisle of wooden chairs, looking for anything she could use as a weapon. "Who are you?" she cried.

"A soldier," he said. "A soldier for France."

CHAPTER FIFTEEN

*L*éonie's *fingers closed* over his. She pulled him across the room to a long stone box lying in the corner. To Marius, it looked like a small sarcophagus. "What is that?" he asked.

She whirled and held up her palm. "Can I trust you?"

He stepped forward and pressed his hand to hers. "With anything," he said. "And everything."

She tilted her head and looked into his eyes. "I believe you," she said. Then she dropped to her knees and began clawing at one end of the box.

"Stop it!" he said, dropping down beside her and trying to pull her hands away. "What are you doing? You'll hurt yourself."

But then the stone she scrabbled at came loose.

She wiggled it left and right, teasing it from its resting place.

Marius glanced at the wall behind the box. In the swampy darkness, it looked the same as all the others. But Léonie had said this room bordered the Reverend Mère's cell...and that her Reverend Mère had tasked her with something important. "She hid something, didn't she?"

"She had to." Léonie pulled out the capstone and set it on the floor. She reached one slender arm into the box. Her fingers grasped something metal; it scraped against the stone as she pulled it out. Even in the darkness, he knew what it was.

Léonie stood and raised the sword, clasping the hilt with both hands. The silver blade shone a wan light on her pale brow. It was old and plain, by modern standards. There were no jewels, gold, or ornamentation on the hilt, but it appeared as if there were patterns — hatches, or perhaps crosses — in the blade itself.

He stood up and ran his finger along its edge. "Why this?"

"It belonged to her."

"The Reverend Mère?"

The girl shook her head. "It belonged to Jeanne."

Marius blinked. "Jeanne. You don't mean ... "

"Is there another?"

"*Mon Dieu.*" He stepped backward. "How can this be?"

"Jeanne heard voices, too, you know."

"I do," he said.

"They told her when she was going to be captured, and she sent her possessions home with her brothers to keep them from the hands of the English."

"Why did they care?" He stepped from left to right, taking in the sword from each side. "It looks like an ordinary sword to me."

She closed her eyes and turned her head, as if listening for a sound he couldn't hear. "The voice says they were looking for relics. They wanted everything she had touched to be burned, not just her flesh. They came to her family home, searching, tearing things apart. Her brothers kept this hidden."

"But how did it get here?"

"The Reverend Mère fetched it herself. With all the riots in the provinces, she thought it would be safer here, under her own care."

Marius shook his head. "It cannot be." He thought of all the altars and scepters that claimed to have a splinter of the True Cross. If they were all put together, it would create a forest. "It must be a hoax."

"It isn't." She trailed her hand down the flat of the blade. "I can feel it."

"It's impossible!"

"It came to her with this," she said, lowering the sword and reaching beneath the neck of her tunic. She pulled up a leather thong, twined around a small vial. Her fingertips held it gently, as if it were fragile.

"What is that?"

She held it up. His eyes had adjusted enough to see that the vial contained something dark. As he looked, Léonie tilted it slightly.

The darkness moved.

The vial was full of liquid.

He studied the shape of the vial — a bulb on the bottom tapering to a narrow neck, stoppered with a thick coating of wax. "I don't understand," he said.

"It's her blood."

Marius felt his throat close as he tried to swallow. "Impossible."

"You already said that."

"How do you know that's what it is? Did the Reverend Mère tell you?"

Léonie nodded. "A surgeon cut a bolt out of Jeanne's leg after she tried to take Paris. He was afraid she would die, so he took this as a memento."

"How has it survived all this time?"

"I don't know," Léonie said. "But the Reverend Mère told me she was its last protector."

"And she chose you to follow her."

Léonie blushed. "I don't know why. I usually gathered apples and collected the dirty linens."

Marius's mind began to race. If the story was true, these weren't just artifacts—they were closer to relics. Jeanne d'Arc was a legend in the mists of time, but one that still had the power to move old men to tears. Now, Léonie was holding the only part of Jeanne they would ever possess. "It's a miracle," he said. "God has put them into your keeping."

"No," she said, stepping backward. "It was my Reverend Mère."

"We have to tell someone. We have to get them out of here, somewhere they'll be safe."

She hefted the sword in her right hand. "We tell no one."

Marius watched her hand. The sword didn't quiver in her grip. "All right," he said softly, holding up both hands. "We tell no one. But…" He looked up at her in alarm. She was one person, and the conflagration outside was burning fiercely all around them. "I am afraid for you."

"Why?"

"Look what they are doing to us," he said. "This revolution wants nothing of the ancien régime left to remind us of what used to be. They are dismantling the church and imprisoning us for no crime other than obedience to God. This is not something we can stop, Léonie. Your voice doesn't even think I'll live another month. What will happen to you then?"

"You won't die," she said, shaking her head. "I won't let you."

A tremor shook his heart and he smiled. "Grown attached to me, I see?"

Léonie nodded. He'd meant it as a jest, but her gray eyes filled with tears.

"Hush," he said. "We'll think of something. I won't leave you."

She set the sword down on its sarcophagus. "I'm scared."

"As am I."

"Why have they locked you and your brothers in here? Why did they kill the Reverend Mère? What did they do with the rest of my sisters? What did we do that God sees fit to punish us? You said this is because we have no other way to prove ourselves to him, but why must He be so cruel?"

"He isn't cruel," Marius said, reaching for her. He remembered the comfort she had found in their kiss, and wanted to give her that comfort again. He let his fingers slide through the tips of her shorn hair. "You must never believe that."

"Then why?"

"Because He isn't here right now."

"That's what you believe?" she said softly.

"I have to," he said, sliding his hand through her hair once more. "Or I have to believe that the Prussians, the Jacobins, the burning, the looting, and the killing are all part of His plan for us. I can't do that."

"He is gone," she whispered, her gaze sinking to the floor. "Was He ever here?"

"Yes," he said, tilting her chin toward him.

"But He is gone now," she said again.

He nodded.

"Then He cannot save us."

He shook his head.

"Or hear us."

He shook his head again.

"Or see us," she whispered, stepping closer to him. She twined her arms around his waist and pressed her lips to his. They were soft and cool, shaking as she held them against his mouth.

In a vivid flash of memory, he felt the sun warm his shoulders as he walked through a wheat field near his father's home. He held out his hand as he walked, letting the gentle stalks caress his palms. When he turned his face to the sun, the softest breeze cooled his brow. He could smell the earth, the wheat, the river, and the air, in perfect harmony. Until this moment, he'd never thought he would feel that sense of perfect calm again. The world was mad and it was doing its damnedest to kill them, but here, with her, he could walk in those gentle fields once more.

She would be his home.

He raised his hands to her shoulders and pulled her closer.

Then he slid his fingertips down her back, reaching for the curve that led to her hips.

Léonie moaned into his mouth. She pulled away and licked her lips. "I don't want to die alone," she whispered.

"Then let me die with you," he said.

She pressed her lips to his again, and he answered with hunger, with fear, and with lust.

CHAPTER SIXTEEN

*N*atalie's *fingers grasped* the back of a wooden chair. The false priest loomed at the other end of the aisle. He stood between her and the chapel's double doors. There was no way she could beat him there, and no other exit point that she could see. *Constantine,* she thought. *I need you.*

But he was in Moscow — no one was coming to rescue her this time.

You'll have to do that yourself, little one, Belial said.

Her panicked heartbeat thumped in her carotid artery. She breathed in through her nose and exhaled through her mouth, like Beth had taught her. Then she looked the false priest in the eye. "What do you want from me?"

"Tell me how you knew about Jeanne."

"I heard her voice, outside the church and again in here."

"Someone must have talked," he growled. "Was it Ricaud?"

He doesn't believe us, little one, Belial said. *But we can make him believe.*

He tapped her with a wing, and a burst of pain flared behind her eyes. Out of the blackness, colors and shapes coalesced. An ocean of sand, blue sky, and a rectangular white hat, blowing across the dunes. *The desert*, she thought. Then that vision dissolved and a new one took its place. This time, she saw a canopy of green leaves, a muddy river, and a snake twined around the trunk of a tree. The snake turned its head and hissed. Blood dripped from its forked tongue.

She cried out and stumbled backward.

The vision faded.

The priest had come three steps closer to her.

She looked at his throat, where she'd seen the thin green line tattooed around his neck. It was the mark of the guillotine, a common criminal's tattoo. *The tattoo*, she thought. *The white hat.* "You're a Légionnaire."

The false priest stopped. "Who are you?"

She stepped backward and bumped into another wooden chair. Its legs scraped against the floor, echoing in the cavernous nave. "No one," she said.

"It took us years to track her," the false priest said. "We know she hid it here. The question is … how did you?"

An artifact, she thought. *They're looking for a religious artifact or a relic.* Something worth sending a soldier dressed as a priest to retrieve. She remembered the rivulets of blood preserved in the shine. Was it something someone had died to protect during the revolution?

You can't let them have it, Belial said.

She looked at the false priest. He'd mentioned the shrine, which meant he'd been upstairs. But he'd found her here in the chapel, downstairs. The last thing someone posing as a priest in a seminary should do is wander around, increasing his chance of getting caught. "You don't know where it is," she said.

The false priest reached into his jacket and pulled out a pistol, aiming it at her heart. "Baptiste said it's in the Rangement. What does your angel say about that?"

Baptiste.

The name sent a shock wave of panic through her veins. Beth was meeting a man with that name at her conference. "Evrard Baptiste?"

The false priest's lips twitched.

Beth, she thought. *Is Beth in trouble, too?* What the hell did a famous professor have to do with a Légionnaire? And if Belial knew something was wrong, why hadn't he said anything before Beth left the hotel? "Why didn't you let me warn her?" she hissed.

She wouldn't have let you out of her sight, Belial said. *I needed you here.*

"Enough!" The false priest strode toward her. He grabbed her right arm, his fingertips digging into her scar. "You will go out the door and up the staircase. Speak to anyone and I will shoot you. Try to run and I will shoot you."

"In a church?"

"I've seen the places God ought to be, and he isn't there. I doubt he's here, either." He dragged her toward the chapel's center aisle and shoved her in front of him. *"Allez."*

Natalie looked over her shoulder at the false priest. He'd slipped his gun hand into his jacket pocket. It was still pointed directly at her. *This can't be happening,* she thought. *Belial, what do I do?*

Do as he asks. He will lead us to it.

To what? she wanted to scream. *What is any of this about?*

"Move." The false priest pushed her forward.

I can't, she thought. *I have to get to Beth. I have to warn her.*

Natalie stumbled toward the chapel door. Her right hand reached for the latch. Her shaking fingers closed around the beaten iron, pressing the flange down. Then she flung the door open, burst through, and dashed around the corner toward the staircase.

A bullet splintered the plastered wall to her right.

She bolted up the stairs, tall cement steps that made her thigh muscles burn.

Another bullet pinged the step below her.

Her frightened breaths echoed the flap of Belial's wings. *Stop!* he cried.

But she couldn't. She reached out with both hands, pressing against the stone walls. The staircase spiraled and she forced her legs to keep moving.

But something clattered behind her.

Then something grabbed her.

She tried to move her feet, but they weren't on a step anymore. They were falling. Now her whole body was falling. When her head struck a stone, everything turned the color of night.

CHAPTER SEVENTEEN

SEPTEMBER 2, 1792
PARIS, FRANCE

Léonie picked up the leather cord attached to the vial of Jeanne d'Arc's blood. Marius watched as she slipped it over her neck and secured the glass beneath the cloth she used to bind her breasts. She only took it off when they lay together.

He had never intended for things to go this far. But once they'd realized they could make the fear go away, if only for a few minutes at a time, they couldn't stop. They didn't *want* to stop. In the aftermath, when they lay tired and damp in each other's arms, the world became a gentle place once more.

The world outside was not a gentle place.

The Prussians had taken Longwy and were marching on Verdun — they were probably already there, in fact. If Verdun fell, there was nothing but forest to keep them from Paris. The revolutionaries in the Assembly expected the Prussians to murder them in their beds. In the chapel below, the men expected the Prussians to set them free. The entire city waited for death or deliverance. No matter which came to them, he wanted to meet his fate with the memory of having loved. One broken vow seemed a small price to pay when the new rulers of France had broken all of them. Today was the sixteenth time in as many days they'd spread their clothes on the stone floor and laid down on them together.

He watched her dress as he lay on floor, fingers crossed over his chest.

"You look like an effigy," she said.

"I am an effigy," he said. "You killed me. I'm dead."

Léonie smiled and knelt, kissing him gently. "It must be time for *déjuner*. Someone will wonder where you are."

"I don't care," he said. "I would rather stay with you."

With Léonie, he had found more than love. He had found purpose — protecting her, protecting Jeanne's relics, and bringing them all to safety somewhere the church could look out for them.

"What are we going to do?" she asked, smoothing her rumpled tunic.

"We can't stay here," he said, standing up to shake the dust from his garments. He dressed quickly. "Whether the Prussians come or not, we have to leave."

"Do you know anyone on the outside?"

"A few of my fellow brothers in Reims, but they're arresting us everywhere. It won't be safe to go to them."

Léonie bit her lip. "I can't go back to mine. They're the ones who gave me up."

"Then we'll be each other's family," he said, tucking the curling ends of her hair behind her ears.

"Even when we get out?"

He kissed her gently. "We leave together, and we stay together. We can pretend to be travelers."

She tilted her head and frowned. "The voice says that's not safe. They'll ask us for papers."

"Then we'll find a way to get papers." His stomach let loose a growl. "I'll go find us some food. While I'm gone, listen at the door. If no one is in the Reverend Mère's cell, try to look out her window into the garden. We need to watch the guards and learn about their patterns."

He stretched his arms and bent from side to side. His back ached from the hours spent on the hard stone, but he would never complain about the feel of Léonie's bare skin next to his. Images from the afternoon flashed through his mind, of their fierce coupling, then their tender one. Only once had he thought of his broken vow. Of all the emotions he felt, shame was not one of them.

"Do you hear that?" Léonie asked.

"Hear what?"

"The voice says they're coming."

"Who?"

Her eyes flew open and her right hand clutched at her chest. "No," she whispered.

He reached out and grasped her arms. "What is it saying?"

"How many?" She brought her hands to her head, pressing the palms against her temples until her arms shook with the pressure. "No, you have to stop them!"

"Tell me what it said!"

"But there's no time!" she shrieked.

"Léonie!"

She clasped him to her, burying her face in his neck. "They're coming for us," she said. "They're coming here."

"Who's coming?"

"A mob, with sticks and axes and pikes. They've massacred the prisoners in St. Germain."

And then he heard it. Through the stone walls, across the courtyard, in the street. It began as a dull roar, a tingle in his ears. Then, as he listened, he began to hear things — screams and strangled cries. The clang of weapons. Shrieks and moans and shouts and the gurgling of blood in a dying man's throat.

"I think they're already here," he said.

CHAPTER EIGHTEEN

PRESENT DAY
PARIS, FRANCE

Maillard grabbed the girl's body and swung it up over his shoulder. Behind him, he heard doors opening and closing as people ventured into the lower corridor.

He scuffed over the blood on the step, where she'd hit her head, and hurried upstairs to the room marked "Rangement." The wooden door was rounded on top, spanned by wrought-iron hinges. He opened it slowly, waiting for the inevitable creak.

It didn't come.

He closed the door behind him, laid the girl on the floor, and dragged a wooden chair under the latch. There was no way to lock it from the inside.

It would have to hold.

If it didn't… well, he'd only shot at her twice. The magazine still had seven rounds.

That was a last resort, though, since Baptiste had told him not to attract attention. It would be easier for everyone if no one discovered the theft until it was too late. The problem was that he couldn't steal the sword until he found it.

He bent down next to the girl. A red gash had opened up on her right temple. Blood forked like lightning as it trailed down her cheek and onto the floor. *I should have hit her,* he thought. It would have been easier to revive her from a punch than from a hard fall against a stone stair.

And he had no doubt he'd need to revive her.

Baptiste would want him to find out how she knew about Jeanne's sword. He didn't believe in God or angels or any of the things she'd talked about. The only reasonable explanation was that she had a boss or an informant — in either case, someone who wanted to beat Baptiste to the sword.

He heard a door close downstairs, followed by footsteps.

Someone was poking around.

The girl had gotten into the stairwell before he started shooting. If he was lucky, the people downstairs would walk out into the hallway, perhaps investigate the chapel, find nothing, and go about their business. The church had no security; the people looking around were likely seminary students, easy targets if it came to that.

Still, it didn't leave much time to find what he'd come for.

His fingers fumbled in his pocket for the burner phone Baptiste had given him.

CHAPTER NINETEEN

"*Let me guess,*" Beth said. "You want to be the shepherd who tells the sheep where to go?"

"I already am," Baptiste said. "You came when I called, didn't you?"

She looked at his thin face and multi-colored hair, a mix of brown and white and gray. *You're not the shepherd,* she wanted to say. *You're the wolf.*

She took a gulp of wine to stifle the impulse to speak. She'd caused enough trouble already. If Baptiste called the university and complained about her, they'd pass her up for department chair again. No one would listen when she told them he was a racist bag of dicks.

"What?" Baptiste said. "No witty comeback, mademoiselle?"

Swear words arranged themselves in a never-ending string of dependent clauses in her head. If she paid it all into the swear jar back home, labeled "Seth's College Fund," the kid's second year of Harvard would be a breeze. But she'd also lose all credibility among her fellow presenters. She swallowed her pride and the last of her wine, batting her eyelashes at Baptiste. "What are you presenting tomorrow?" she asked.

"Theories on the origin, construction, and symbolism of the sword of St. Catherine of Fierbois."

Beth blinked.

The only swords she was familiar with were from legends and cartoons — the one King Arthur pulled from a stone, and the one He-Man lofted as he said, "By the power of Grayskull." She pictured Baptiste in a furry loincloth and had to bite her lip to keep a straight face. "I'm not familiar with that particular sword."

"Allow me," Malone Marchand said, leaning over her shoulder and speaking *sotto voce.* "It was found in the fifteenth century, behind the altar of the church of Saint Catherine of Fierbois in Tours."

Beth turned her head toward him. He smelled of wine, tobacco, and the woods. His presence was warm and comforting, the antidote to Baptiste's prickly egotism. And he wasn't bad to look at, either — tall and olive-skinned, with floppy dark hair like Olivier Martinez circa *The Horseman on the Roof.* "Who found it?"

"None other than Jeanne d'Arc."

"Yes," Baptiste snapped, glaring at Marchand. "An angel told Jeanne to seek out this sword after the dauphin, the future Charles VII, agreed to place her at the head of his army."

"Wait a minute." Beth's fingers clenched around her empty glass. "Did you say an angel told her where to look?"

"I thought you prided yourself on your knowledge of our history, mademoiselle."

"I knew she heard voices. I didn't know they were angels."

"Just one," Marchand said.

"Isn't it always." Then she braced herself for the answer she didn't want to hear. "Did this angel have a name?"

"It was the Archangel Michael who spoke to her."

She let out her breath. "Oh, thank God."

Marchand smiled. "I'm sure that's what Jeanne said, too."

"That sword," Baptiste said, "is the same one Charles Martel carried when he defeated Abdul Rahman and the Muslim invaders at Tours. The power of such a symbol linked Joan with France's most famous defender. Today, that sword would speak even louder as a national symbol of unity."

Yves Collard curled his lip. "Can it speak Arabic?"

"Wait." Marchand held out his hand, looking from Collard to Baptiste. "Surely you don't believe the Fierbois sword belonged to Charles Martel. That was a myth, invented by Joan's supporters after her death."

"It is the truth!" Baptiste said. "It belonged to Charles, and then Jeanne. It's still out there now, waiting to be found by the next savior of France."

"You sound like a treasure hunter," said Marchand.

"Do I?" Baptiste snapped. "I'll tell your—"

A phone buzzed in Baptiste's pocket. He stalked away from their awkward cluster to stand near the exit.

She looked up at Marchand. "Is he always such a blast at parties?"

"More," he said, clinking his glass against hers. "You've done very well for your first time. Although you haven't made him swear at you or threaten to knock you down, which is what happened to me the first time I met him."

"Then here's to round two."

Marchand reached into his pocket and pulled out a card. "Please call to make sure I'm there. I would be disappointed beyond belief if I missed it."

"Deal," Beth said, taking the card. She looked sideways at Marchand as she slipped it into her bag. *Good hair*, she thought. *Fantastic bone structure, very well dressed, no wedding ring. He probably turns into a pumpkin at midnight.*

She looked away before he could catch her checking him out. This time, her gaze settled on Baptiste. His knuckles and his face had gone white.

"What's that all about?" she whispered to Marchand, jerking her head in Baptiste's direction. "I don't suppose you can read lips."

"I can try," he said, inching closer and whispering into her ear. "What do you mean, you don't have it?" Marchand paused. "You did what?"

"Someone's gonna get it," she said.

Marchand closed the gap between them. His wine-scented breath moved her hair against her neck and she shivered. "Find it," he said. "Find it now."

"I'm enjoying this way more than I should."

Marchand brushed her ear with his lips. "She knows nothing. *Tu es bête comme tes pieds.*"

"A little help with that last part?"

"He is insulting whoever is speaking. Oh, that's interesting."

Beth groaned and leaned into Marchand. "Don't hold out on me now."

"She doesn't speak to angels. She doesn't know anything. It's not possible. Just shut her up and do your job."

The wine glass slipped from her hand.

The other professors gasped, and the sound drew Baptiste's attention. He said something else and hung up.

"Are you all right?" Marchand asked, bending to pick up her glass as it rolled harmlessly on the thick carpet. "Doctor Brandon?"

"I have to go," she said, hoisting her purse strap over her shoulder.

CHAPTER TWENTY

"We have to stay in here," Léonie said, clutching at his robe. "The things the voice says…" She shook her head. "We cannot stop it."

She flinched as the air filled with the sound of a crash, followed by the splintering of wood.

"The garden door," Marius said softly. "They've forced their way in." He put his arm around her. "I came in through the passageway. Where is the door that leads to your Reverend Mère's cell?"

"No!" Léonie cried. "We have to stay here."

"If they're getting in, perhaps we can get out." He held his palm against her cheek. "I told you I would get you out of this place."

Léonie turned to kiss his palm. "I'm so scared."

"I am, too. But that doesn't mean we shouldn't try." He tilted her head down to kiss her forehead. "Please, Léonie ... show me the door."

She nodded and wiped away a tear. Without a word, she slid the sword box out from against the far wall and dragged her fingers across a seam of mortar. "It's here," she said, pushing it open. A beam of light from the Reverend Mère's cell burst into the darkness.

Marius squinted and held his hand to his eyes. "Stay here," he said, crouching in the doorway. "I'll be back soon."

Léonie ignored him, following close on his heels as he slipped through the door.

He reached one hand back, secretly glad for the company, and she took it.

He led her to the cell's only window and they peered out into the garden.

Hands appeared at the top of the outer wall. They grasped the creeping vines and pulled, producing their owners' elbows, shoulders, and red-capped heads. Men began to fall over the wall and drop into the garden. In their hands they held axes, knotty clubs, and sticks. Some stood up slowly, their bodies damaged by the fall.

Others in loose pants and red caps flooded through the ruptured garden door, brandishing pikes, clubs, cutlasses, and pistols. From every direction, armed men marched toward the chapel, windmilling weapons in wild practice swings. "Take the oath!" they shouted. "Swear or die!"

The invaders split into two packs, the largest marching down the graveled path that divided the garden into parterres. "Look!" Léonie said, pointing a few meters ahead of the marching men.

A priest in a black robe knelt, his hands pressed together as his lips moved in prayer. The man at the head of the pack lifted a sabre and brought it down over his head, nearly splitting it in two. Blood and gore streamed down the priest's shoulders and his body toppled to the ground. The men with pikes stepped forward, raising them high and stabbing the lifeless body.

Léonie screamed.

Marius pulled her to him, covering her mouth with his hand. "Don't," he said. "There's nothing we can do for him."

The second pack of invaders had veered left. At the foot of the garden, near the boundary walls, sat a stone oratory. Its only decoration was a worm-eaten wooden carving of the Blessed Virgin. Two benches had been placed in front of it for prayer. A group of priests was caught there, between the invaders and the garden walls. One man stepped forward and held out his arms, as if to protect the men behind him.

"Who is that man?" he asked.

Léonie tilted her head and squinted. "The Archbishop of Arles," she whispered. "Marius, don't look. The voice says …" But she couldn't say it.

He kept his arms around her, ready to stifle another scream. The man Léonie's voice identified as the archbishop said something. Then a man struck him on the head with a cutlass. The archbishop staggered. A second blow laid his skull open. He raised his hands to shield himself and the third blow hacked off his left hand at the wrist.

Two men stepped forward.

"No," Léonie whispered.

One man stabbed a pike into the archbishop's belly. The other used his pike to impale the severed hand.

Léonie turned her head into his chest. Her small fingers dug into his arm.

Marius looked away from the stream of blood already pooling under the archbishop's body.

That's when something caught his eye — something dark scuttling up the far left garden wall, on the other side of the chapel.

One of the priests had run.

He held his breath as he watched the man try to climb, reaching for vines and scrambling for a foothold. Could he get Léonie, the sword, and the vial across the garden and over the wall without being caught?

The invaders were spreading out, herding the priests in the garden like sheep. He heard a shot, saw a puff of smoke, and one of the brown-robed figures fell. Two more quick shots and the dark figure climbing the far wall fell to the ground, dark patches staining his robe.

The bread and apple he'd eaten last night threatened to come up as he watched the terrified priests in the garden huddle together. *I should be with them,* he thought. *I should show my brothers I'm not afraid to die with them. I should show my God I am not afraid to die for Him.*

Then he looked at Léonie.

But I want to live, he thought.

"Léonie," he said. "Open your eyes."

She did as he asked. Even with tears gleaming in reddened eyes, she was beautiful.

"We're going to live," he said.

She said nothing.

"We're going down to the chapel. I will find us a way out." He pressed a kiss to her forehead. "Gather your things."

She nodded, crawling back through the secret door. Images flooded his mind of what they had done there. A whisper of doubt pricked his soul. Had he marked himself as unworthy by betraying his vows? What if his sin doomed them both?

No, he told himself. *She needed someone, and God sent me to her.*

He took a deep breath to quell the unrest in his gut and followed her into the chamber. Scraps of burlap and twine lay on the stone floor, where they'd left them after last night's meal. *The sword*, he thought.

His fingers scrambled to pick up the lengths of twine and began tying them together. There would be enough; her waist was small. "Here," he said, holding up the length of twine, now dotted with knots. "Tie the sword around your waist, under your tunic."

She nodded and reached for her hem. He tried to glance away from the white legs beneath her tunic. He couldn't.

Her fingers worked more quickly than his. She wound the twine around her waist and knotted the ends around the handle of the sword. "Done," she said, dropping her tunic over the blade.

"That sounded confident," he said.

"The voice told me we'll make it to the chapel."

"And after that?"

She bit her lip. "He growled at me and turned his back."

"Tell your voice I don't care what happens to me. I would die here gladly, protecting you with my last breath. Tell him he need only speak of you."

Her forehead furrowed and he knew the voice was speaking to her once more. *Lie to her if you must,* he begged the voice. *But give her courage. Give her strength.*

His own fear was beginning to spread and take hold, like fever or plague. Thoughts of blood and bone and pain and death were waiting in the shadows of his mind, ready to overtake him. If he let them, he would be a danger to Léonie. The only thought that frightened him more than his bodily pain was hers. "Are you ready?" he asked, pulling her cowl over her hair.

Léonie nodded.

He took her hand and led her out of the secret chamber. "Stay behind me."

"No." She moved to stand at his side, gray eyes staring back at him, unblinking.

He kissed her once, hard and fast. Then, fingers laced, they descended the narrow staircase that led from the Reverend Mère's cell to the sacristy.

The air thrummed with fear and sweat and panic and prayer. Rough voices echoed against the limestone walls: "Death to the refractory!" and "Take the oath!"

In the distance, the din of clanking weapons echoed like machinery.

At the foot of the staircase, Marius pressed himself to the wall and Léonie did the same. He twisted his torso to glance around the corner into the chapel. It was full of his brothers, flooding toward the altar steps, as far from the garden and chapel entrance as they could get. A handful of uniformed National Guards patrolled both sides of the chapel's open doors.

He wanted to believe the guards were a good sign. They had been sent to protect them, hadn't they? To keep order and prevent the villains in the garden from murdering them all? But if that were true, why weren't they helping the men being killed in the garden?

Marius shook his head. Everything was upside down and underwater and on fire at the same time.

"Inside!" barked two of the guards at the entrance, facing the garden. "Get inside now, all of you! It's time for roll-call!"

He gulped. The sans-culottes outside would chase the men who ran inside. Chaos would have been their ally, but once every pair of eyes was focused on the chapel, there was no hope.

He had to find another way out.

The roof, he thought. They could climb out the window in the Reverend Mère's cell.

"Come," he said, grabbing Léonie's hand.

"Hey, you there!" a voice called behind them. "You, on the stairs!"

Léonie froze.

"Don't stop," he said. "The Reverend Mère's cell. *Allez, allez, vite!*"

Léonie answered with a burst of speed as they fled up the staircase hand-in-hand.

His only thought was of the door to the secret room — he'd left it open. If they could get in and get it closed before the guardsman caught up with them, they had a chance.

He heard the clamor in the chapel as a guardsman shouted after them.

It's no use, he thought. *They'll give chase.*

Léonie rounded the corner at the top of the landing.

He glanced over his shoulder. The shuffle of boots wasn't far behind. He squeezed her hand and let it go, brushing the small of her back with his outstretched fingers. "Go," he whispered.

Then he turned to face the guardsman alone.

CHAPTER
TWENTY-ONE

eth hurried across the room toward Evrard Baptiste. He saw her coming and fled through the ballroom's double doors.

"Wait!" she cried.

She didn't catch him until he was outside the vestibule, in the hotel hallway. Thick burgundy carpet muffled the sound of her footsteps. She reached out and grabbed his arm, pulling with all her weight. "Wait."

"I don't have time for this, Mademoiselle Brandon," he said, glaring at her hand.

"I heard what you said...about the angel. What was that about?"

He jerked his arm out of her grasp. "I'm leaving now. If you know what's good for you, you'll do the same."

"I need to know," she said, stepping in front of him.

"I owe you nothing. Get out of my way."

"I know who she is."

Baptiste stopped. She felt his eyes on her, seeing her as more than a nuisance for the first time. The fear in her gut was temporarily numbed by a burst of satisfaction.

"Who are you?" he hissed.

She stared back at him, looking for the spark in his eyes that would tell her what she wanted to know. She remembered the cold fire of Prime Minister Maxim Starinov's eyes, oblivious to reality. She remembered the dead-eyed stare of his Vympel men, oblivious to humanity. Baptiste's eyes were cold like Starinov's, but without the delusion. Instead, there was a detached curiosity, something both Starinov and the Vympel men lacked. "I was about to ask you the same question."

Baptiste's lips curled in a lupine smile. "It's not polite to eavesdrop, mademoiselle. You will regret it."

"I don't think so," Beth said. "Now tell me what the hell you're doing with my sister."

"Sister," Baptiste said softly. "Things are about to go very badly for you, mademoiselle."

"*About* to? Do you have any idea what happened to us last summer? If you think you can fuck up my life any more than those guys, take your best shot."

Baptiste's right fist launched a haymaker straight into her chin.

CHAPTER TWENTY-TWO

The darkness began to flicker. Black and white light streamed before her eyes like a film reel.

Wait, Natalie thought. *Darkness doesn't flicker.*

Of course not, Belial said. *You're still sleeping.*

A flash of light went off in her head. It took her a moment to realize that flash was the last thing she remembered. *I don't think I was sleeping.*

You are, Belial said. *Because there are things I should have told you.*

Things about what? she asked.

The angel hung his head. *That September, His back was turned. They lived in shadow, breathing darkness and despair. You cannot imagine how they felt.*

And then she remembered. She'd been in the chapel of Saint-Joseph-des-Carmes, steps away from where more than a hundred priests had been massacred. As terrible a thing as it was, she still didn't know what it had to do with her, or why Belial had brought her here.

You don't understand, Belial said.

That's what I've been trying to tell you my whole life, she thought.

Then I must make you see.

A wave of heat and nausea overtook her. The blackness of her dreamscape burned away and she saw the church's soaring cupola. Then she looked down and saw the chapel itself, full of men in dark robes. They huddled near the altar and whispered, eyes darting anxiously from side to side. Some slid sweat-soaked rosaries through swollen fingers.

Somewhere nearby, a church bell rang — once, twice, three times, four times. She heard something else, too. It filled the air, shrieking through the chapel's limestone façade, slipping through everything made by the hands of men. It was the sky. It was screaming, choking on blood, gargling with sulfur. *The devil's trill,* Belial said. *May you never live to hear it.*

What does it mean? she asked.

But Belial didn't answer her.

"Into the line," a rough voice said. "Time for roll-call."

A man in a red cap, his face smeared with blood, pushed a few brown-robed men against the chapel wall. The men trudged to the end of a long line, snaking its way toward a short, dim hallway.

That hallway led to a set of doors that opened onto the garden. In front of the doors, a man with an aquiline nose and amber eyes stood behind a table, holding a splintered club. Two henchmen escorted the priest at the head of the line to stand before him. The priest wept and recited the Ave Maria.

"State your name," the dark-eyed man said.

The priest didn't answer. One of the men beside him prodded him with a pike. "A — Ambroise-Augustin," he mumbled, returning immediately to his prayer.

"You are charged with treason, choosing to serve the one named God instead of our sovereign state. How do you plead?"

The priest recited faster, desperate to reach the end of the prayer. He finished, crossed himself, and looked at the amber-eyed man. "Y — you are forgiven," he said.

"And you are guilty," the judge replied, bashing the table with his club in place of a gavel.

The men beside him pushed him out the doorway, down three small stairs into the garden.

A man with an axe took off the priest's head.

Natalie screamed.

No one heard her.

The devil had stolen all the air.

In the garden, strewn beyond the fallen body, she saw dozens more dead and dying. Angry men in blood-soaked clothes swung swords and cutlasses, splitting heads like logs. The ones without weapons tussled like dogs, pulling tug-of-war on the dying men's arms and legs. They pulled until the robed men came apart. Men with sharpened sticks prised up body parts and slid them onto their pikes, jousting with stacks of hearts or hands.

"Next," said the judge. He banged the gavel and spattered himself with blood.

The stench of sweat and blood clogged her throat. She had never seen a person inside out before. "Stop it, Belial!" she screamed.

You wish me to be kind? The way the world was kind to these men? I have not shown you the worst, little one.

She woke up screaming.

"Shh," a familiar voice said. "It's all right, babe."

Natalie gasped for breath and flailed. The vision dissolved into the familiar limestone walls, but she didn't want to see it, not anymore. The air inside the church was cold, and now she knew why.

"Nat, can you hear me?"

"Beth?" She moved her head and discovered she was lying in her sister's lap, blood from her temple all over Beth's slacks. In the corner of the room, two men stood together, their backs to her, in whispered conference. "What are you doing here? What's going on?"

"Baptiste," Beth growled, glaring at one of the men. "He socked me."

"They're looking for some kind of artifact. I don't know what it is."

"What did he do to you?" Beth asked, smoothing the hair away from her bleeding temple.

On cue, the Légionnaire turned to glare at them. His face looked like exactly like the man in her nightmare. "You were there!" she said, pointing at him.

Beth grabbed her hand and tried to press it down. "Not a good time, babe."

"I saw you!" she cried. "You were the one with the gavel."

This time, the second man turned around. "Gavel?"

Natalie recognized him from the author photo on the books in Beth's office. He looked older and thinner, with more gray hair. "Doctor Baptiste," she said. "It would be an honor not to meet you."

He crossed the room toward her, head tilted in inquiry. "Why did you mention a gavel?"

Natalie stared up at him. His eyes were small and distant, as if he were looking at her under a microscope. "If you're asking me, it means you already know."

"Monsieur Maillard has told me some very interesting things about you."

"Did he tell you I like whiskey? That's probably all you need to know."

"He did not."

"What do you want with us?"

"I think you know," he said, kneeling to face her. "You wouldn't be here otherwise."

"I'm here because of Belial," she said, looking up at Beth. "He said there is a great evil in this place. That there was something here connected to our bloodline."

"And you listened to him?"

"He said he'd protect Seth if I did what he wanted."

"You manipulative motherfucker," Beth said. "I know you can hear me in there, you feathered asshole."

I hear her, Belial said. *Tell her she'll be sorry in a year or so.*

Natalie shook her head and instantly regretted it. She could no longer tell which hurt worse — Belial's movements or her fall against the staircase. She sucked in her breath and focused on Baptiste. "Belial knows what you're searching for."

"If he knows where to find it, I'm sure Monsieur Maillard would appreciate the help."

Baptiste looked over his shoulder at Maillard, who had pulled a small rectangular device from his jacket pocket. He had already moved the Madonna and Child statue out of the way. He held up the device against the wall beside the blood shrine, and began moving it up and down. A digital screen displayed an image that looked like an X-ray, with pipes and wires illuminated in different colors.

Metal, Natalie thought. She'd thought they were looking for a religious artifact that had belonged to the Reverend Mère — paper, bone, hair, fabric, that sort of thing. Had the Reverend Mère hidden coins or jewels instead? What could be worth kidnapping and assaulting two foreign citizens in order to find?

Her eyes drifted toward the shrine. Belial had brought her to it on the very day Baptiste and Maillard were attempting to steal something from the church. There had to be a connection. Whose blood was in the shrine? Someone who'd defended the treasure?

Someone who did more than that, Belial said.

"Regardez-moi." Baptiste grabbed her chin and jerked it toward him. "It took me thirty years to find it. Thirty years of reading and research, of travel and dead ends and sleepless nights. I have crossed the length and breadth of my country in search of it, for longer than you have been alive, and yet here you are. Tell me, mademoiselle … how did you know where to look?"

His fingers snaked their way up her cheekbones, tracing them as if he were drawing them. Then they squeezed her face until her teeth cut into her cheek. "Tell me now, and if you prove yourself useful, I may let you live."

A high-pitched beep echoed against the far wall.

Baptiste spun on his knee, his hand still gripping her cheeks. Maillard stood to the right of the shrine, holding the device at ankle level. *"Ici,"* he said.

Baptiste turned back with a smile. "It appears I don't need you after all. Modern technology trumps your … angel." He shoved her back into Beth's arms and rose to his feet. From the opposite corner of the room, he retrieved a black zip-top bag, hammer, and pickaxe.

"You start hammering on that plaster," Beth said, "and someone will come running."

"You have a poor opinion of me," Baptiste said, pulling out a cheap flip phone, "if you think I would allow that to happen."

He dialed and spoke rapid French to the person on the other end of the line. Natalie closed her eyes and tried to pick out as many words as she could. There was only one she needed: *bombe.*

"Real original," she said. "Who gave you the idea, a sophomore who didn't feel like taking your midterm?"

"It won't work," Beth added. "The bomb squad will have to clear every room in the building, and the cops will set up a perimeter. There's nowhere to hide."

Baptiste glared at them. "A very poor opinion, indeed."

You cannot let him have it, Belial said. *He will use it in order to kill.*

"Belial says you want to kill," she repeated. "Who's on your hit list?"

Baptiste cleared his throat. His eyes seemed to look past her, through the wall, into a place that didn't even exist. "'Never, by God, for my misdeed shall kinsmen hear the blame, nor sweet France fall into evil fame. Felon pagans are gathered to their shame. I pledge you now, to death they're doomed today.'"

His voice snapped an image to her mind — a book cover, something from her father's library. On it was a painting of a mounted knight in helmet and hauberk, holding aloft his sword, blood streaming down his face. Under his rearing horse's hooves were dead men wearing turbans. "The Song of Roland," she said.

Beth groaned. "You want to kill Muslims. I *knew* you were a racist bag of dicks."

Maillard spun, flinging the metal detector to the floor. He stalked up to Beth and spat at her. "My father was killed by a Muslim terrorist, a coward who set a bomb on a train and walked away. They murdered my father, who bled for his country in the sands of *Algérie*. My father, who went to prison for defending *les pieds-noirs* against Muslim terrorists.

He would have given his life for this country, and this country spit in his face."

"You won't make it right by killing again."

Maillard pulled up his shirt, revealing a scar across his right side. "Is that why we were sent into Afghanistan to hunt Osama bin Laden for you? So you could scold him for what he had done?" He dropped the hem of his shirt. "Tell me what's wrong with killing those who hurt the ones you love."

"Tell me how hating someone you don't know makes anything in this world better."

Natalie narrowed her eyes.

Something was wrong with the words Baptiste had spoken. She could still see the pages in her father's book. Her memory scrolled through them as if it were watching a movie, until she found the lines he had quoted. But her picture had one more line, a line he'd skipped. Why? She closed her eyes and leaned into Beth's arms, willing the words on the page to take shape in her mind. "Belial, help me see it," she whispered.

Durendal, Belial replied. *He did not speak of Durendal.*

In the poem, Durendal was Roland's sword. But why would Baptiste omit the line of the poem mentioning the mythical warrior's sword? A knight wasn't a knight without his sword.

Baptiste yanked Maillard away from Beth. "Get back to work. And you," he said, pointing at Beth, "I expected more from you, mademoiselle. A historian, of all people, should understand why this must be done."

"This is crazy," Beth said. "Just because someone prays to a different god doesn't mean they're out to get you."

He smiled. "'But what avail in prayer? No good there is in that. They are not in time; too long have they held back.'"

"You want to play medieval bullshit bingo?" Beth snapped. "Fine. How about 'Prudence is worth more than stupidity. Here are Franks dead, all for your trickery.' Word to your mother, asshole."

Natalie dug her fingernails into her palm. A wave of heat crested in her veins and she remembered standing in the sunlight outside the wooden doors that led into the church. That was where she'd first heard it — the voice that was not hers and was not Belial. There was only one reason she could think of why he would have brought that particular voice to her. Joan had never been here — even Belial couldn't rewrite history like that. But maybe there was something else of hers here … something that required a metal detector to find.

"The sword," Natalie said. "You found it, didn't you?"

Baptiste handed the small pickaxe to Maillard. "So you've finally decided to tell the truth."

"I won't let you have it."

I knew you'd come around, Belial said.

"Oh, but you will," Baptiste said, pulling a pistol from his waistband. "What better rallying cry to bring my sleeping brothers and sisters to arms? Make no mistake, we are at war. This is a crusade far more important than any we have undertaken before."

"At least have the courage to kill using your own name. Don't hide behind hers."

"Hers?" Beth asked.

"Joan of Arc."

Beth twitched behind her. "That's what this is about? The conference, your presentation…you wanted to be the star of the show, with something to bring to show and tell?"

Baptiste glared at her. "If you think that is all I wanted, you are small-minded, indeed."

Natalie shook her head. "You aren't anything like Joan. She was fighting for her country, for her king. You're fighting for hatred."

"I'm fighting with hatred," Baptiste said. "It's the only weapon they understand."

"I don't believe this," Beth said. "Go to Paris, they said. Give a talk, they said. It'll be fun."

"Strictly speaking, they fight with bombs, cell phones, IEDs, and planes," Natalie said. "You're bringing a sword to a drone fight."

"Then it had better be the right sword," Baptiste said, turning back to Maillard. "Are you ready?"

Natalie glared at his back. "Beth," she whispered, "we can't let them have that sword. If they find it, we have to take it and run like hell."

"I'm not going Butch and Sundance on this. I have a kid, for Christ's sake."

"They're going to kill us once they find it."

"How do you know that?"

"Because it's what I'd do in their place."

"Shit." Beth sighed. "Well, there are two of us and two of them."

Natalie smiled. "Whose ass do you want to kick?"

CHAPTER TWENTY-THREE

SEPTEMBER 2, 1792
PARIS, FRANCE

The guardsman dashed toward him, followed by three sans-culottes. Marius gulped as one of the sans-culottes stretched out a blood-soaked hand and pulled on the guardsman's arm. "Wait," the man growled. "This one's ours."

The guardsman held his rifle sideways to block the staircase. His eyes flickered briefly to Marius's before turning back to the sans-culottes. "There was to be no bloodshed," the guard said. "By order of the Legislative Assembly."

"We do not do things your way," the sans-culotte said. The two men behind him raised their pikes and, over their companion's shoulders, aimed at the guardsman's chest. "Keep these sheep in line, boys. It's almost time for shearing."

The guardsman's eyes roved over the three sans-culottes. Marius knew what he was thinking — one bayonet against three pikes and a swell of bloodlust. The guardsman turned his head to meet Marius's eyes. He blinked once, then pressed his lips in farewell.

Marius did the same. *I understand*, he wanted to say.

The guardsman descended past the sans-culottes, back to the chapel and the roll-call of a hundred doomed men.

The sans-culotte turned. "Keep marching," he jeered. "Straight to the gallows."

Now, Marius thought.

He bolted, dashing up the last two steps, then onto the landing and down the hallway.

Léonie stood at the door of the Reverend Mère's cell.

"*La chambre, vite!*" he called.

He saw a flash of brown as she whirled and dashed for the secret chamber. He raced after her, heart pounding.

He flew into the cell, fingers grasping at the doorframe to redirect his momentum.

The chamber's stone door was still open. Léonie was already inside, out of sight. He bent low, ready to hurl himself through head-first. *God wants us to live*, he thought.

Then he felt two hands grasp his shoulders. The weight of a body hit him and knocked him to the floor. The body rolled off quickly, and he turned onto his back.

"What have you got in there?" a sans-culotte said, holding a pike aimed at his heart.

A second sans-culotte, the man who had tackled him, rose to his feet. "Maybe it's gold. All these bastard priests have gold hidden somewhere."

Marius stared, dazed. His panting breath roared in his ears, drowning out a sudden ringing. The point of the pike hovered less than a hand's width from his beating heart.

The sans-culotte raised his right hand.

He held up his hands as if he could stop the thrust of the pike. The words of a prayer flew through his mind, too fast for his lips to grasp them. *You must forgive them,* he thought. And then, *No, I cannot.*

Suddenly, something quick and bright flashed above him and the sans-culotte groaned.

Marius moved his hands from his face in time to see Léonie pull back her blade. It made a sickly sucking sound, pulling with it blood and gore from the sans-culotte's belly. The man moaned, retched, and dropped his pike. He looked down at his wound and then back to Léonie, mouth agape.

"You will not take the things I love," she hissed as the man fell to the floor. "Only God can do that." She settled into her stance and clasped the hilt with both hands. Then she pointed the tip of her sword at the second sans-culotte. "Are you God?"

The second sans-culotte turned and ran as drops of warm, wet blood fell from her blade.

Léonie held her pose as he scrambled to his feet, until the footsteps of the fleeing sans-culotte had clattered down the hallway. With one hand, he reached out for her, pausing a single breath away from her slanted cheekbone.

"Pick up the pike," she said, turning to face the doorway.

CHAPTER TWENTY-FOUR

*N*atalie *shifted her* weight and leaned sideways to inspect Maillard's progress. In twenty minutes, he'd chipped away the plaster over a section of wall about five feet high and three feet wide, revealing the original limestone blocks beneath.

A safe, she thought. *They're looking for a safe.*

She glanced at Beth, sitting cross-legged beside her. Her sister's palms were pressed flat to the floor. Blue veins stood out like ladders on the backs of her hands. Her eyes were fixed on Baptiste's shoulder blades.

She's decided where to place the knife, Belial said.

"We don't have a knife," she muttered. "Do we?"

Baptiste spun. "No words," he hissed, raising his pistol and pointing it at her face. The pupils of his eyes had dilated. A bead of sweat rolled down his temple.

Natalie watched his hand. Despite his excitement, it didn't shake.

For a moment, all she could hear was the scuffle and muted voices of the seminary students as they evacuated the lower level. Someone outside had a loudspeaker; they were directing the evacuees as they exited the building. The flashing lights of parked police vehicles strobed through the only window, washing the room in blue and white. Their flicker added to the ache throbbing behind her temple.

She looked at Maillard, holding a hammer in one hand and a chisel in the other. *It can't be a safe*, she realized. He wouldn't be able to open it, not without carting it out of the building or blowing it up first.

She narrowed her eyes and looked again at the rectangular outline he'd chipped away.

As a schoolgirl, Beth had taken her to several nearby missions — Mission Dolores, San Rafael Archangel, San Francisco Solano. When they'd toured the outbuildings and sacristies, Beth's immovable Aqua Net bangs had touched the tops of all the doorframes. "People were shorter then," Beth had said. "I don't know what Napoleon was bitching about."

It's not a safe, she realized. *It's a door.*

But a door was much easier to open than a safe. Maillard would pry it open in a few minutes tops, and then what? Baptiste couldn't let them go. The first thing they'd do was tell the media what he'd done, and what his true intentions were.

Baptiste held the gun steady, still pointed at her nose. Veins streaked the whites of his eyes. Would he really shoot them? Not Beth, she thought. He didn't like her, but some part of him clearly wanted acceptance from a fellow academic. No, Maillard was the one to fear. He had much less to lose. His father was the only person whose respect he seemed to crave, and he was already dead — no help there. Plus, he knew how to fight and she didn't. She'd only survived in Russia because Constantine was a soldier — and he'd believed in her.

Belial brushed her with a wing. *Have you forgotten the time I helped, too?*

Yes, she lied.

It wasn't something she ever wanted to remember. During one attack, Belial had taken control of her nervous system, directing her movements and blacking out her vision. He made her do things she would never have done if she were in control, things she'd only sensed through a velvet curtain of darkness. Once again, it had been Constantine who helped her through it.

But you survived, the angel said, his voice sharp with anger. *You are alive because of me.*

She looked down at the scars on her forearms. *I'm alive in spite of you,* she thought.

After all I have done for your family...

You almost destroyed my family, she thought.

I saved it, little one. I saved you.

No one can save me, she thought.

Part of her wished she'd died in the hospital when Belial first appeared, back in fourth grade. Had she been so broken on the inside that nothing but an angel could put her soul back together? How could a little girl even be that broken? If it weren't for Beth, she'd think she was the nightmare and Belial was real. People said time and space were like fabric, rippling and folding and wrinkling. But who held the fabric? Who smoothed it in places and crumpled it in others? The folds didn't know. The ripples couldn't see what was on the other side. *I don't know who I am*, she thought.

I am you, Belial said. *You are me. We are together, little one. Forever.*

The doctors had never understood why she listened to an angel instead of to them. But it was because the pills they'd given her made her forget who Beth was, what her own name was, why she had hair on her head. She'd cut it all off once after a doctor prescribed a new anti-psychotic regimen. Then she slept on the pile of hair for three days straight, until Beth came and found her and threw it away.

Beth.

The only reason to fight, to stay alive, was to make sure Beth did, too.

She had to save her sister.

She had to get back to Constantine.

There were still good things in this world. If she didn't believe that, everything was lost.

The sword, Belial prodded. His wingtip brushed the side of her skull, lighting it up like a pinball machine with bolts of pain and electricity.

I know, she thought.

She couldn't leave Joan's sword with Baptiste. He would turn something pure into a symbol of hatred. Besides, Joan had heard voices, too. Protecting Joan from Baptiste felt right, as if she were protecting herself. It was easier to stand up for Joan, who had turned the tide of a war, than it was to stand up for herself against the doctors.

Good, Belial said. *You are beginning to understand, the way she did.*

"Who?" Natalie asked.

My beautiful Léonie, Belial said. *The last to see and wield the sword.*

"When?"

When innocent blood was spilled.

"The massacre," she whispered. But that didn't make sense. Léonie was a woman's name, and she'd thought only priests were murdered here.

Beth covered Natalie's hand with hers. "What's going on?"

"I said no words!" Baptiste wrapped one finger around the trigger and swerved, aiming at Beth's forehead. "Who is she talking to?"

"You don't want to know. The last guy who asked … let's just say it didn't end well."

"Keep her quiet or I'll find a new use for my hammer and chisel."

Beth inched closer to Natalie, wrapping her arms around her and pulling her near. "Shh," Beth said, her eyes on Baptiste. Then, into Natalie's ear, she whispered, "We have to run."

She tucked her head against Beth's neck and whispered back. "Not without the sword."

Across the room, Maillard's fingers scraped over the limestone blocks, pushing at various points. Baptiste stepped toward him, giving rapid directions in French. His right hand, holding the gun, began to droop.

Natalie leaned forward.

Not yet, little one, Belial said. *Let him bring it to you.*

"Get ready," she whispered, shifting her weight.

A siren wailed outside.

Beth dropped her hands to her sides and untucked her feet. Natalie looked sideways at her sister. *Please let me be right about Baptiste*, she thought. *Please don't let him hurt her.*

"I have it!" Maillard said, tracing a line with his finger. "Look — the mortar is thicker here."

"Push on the edges," Baptiste ordered.

Maillard splayed his fingers over the stone and pushed. A section of wall pivoted inward.

"Push harder!"

Maillard put his shoulder against the panel and pushed. The swollen stones grated against each other, but obeyed. A rectangular panel swiveled open, a portal of inky darkness.

"Holy shit," Beth said.

Natalie pressed her hands to the floor, muscles tensed and waiting.

"Go," Baptiste said. "Now."

Maillard pulled his own pistol from a shoulder holster. He held it in front of him with a double-handed grip. As he moved forward, he swept the gun from left to right. A moment later, he called out to Baptiste. "One room, no other exit. It's clear."

Natalie curled her legs beneath her.

Hold, Belial said.

"Come out," Baptiste barked. "Watch them. If they move, shoot them."

Maillard ducked and emerged from the darkness, a sheen of sweat illuminating his forehead. He wiped his brow with his left hand and smeared wet fingerprints on his pants. Then he aimed his pistol at her heart. *"Allons enfants de la patrie,"* he said, smiling.

Baptiste clapped him on the shoulder as he ducked through the secret door. Natalie heard a click, then saw a pale beam of light. Baptiste swung the flashlight from side to side, floor to ceiling. *"Mon Dieu,"* he said.

A telltale click echoed inside the chamber, followed by the sound of stone scraping against stone. Natalie glanced at Beth. Her sister nodded. She'd also recognized the sound of a gun being laid down.

"It cannot be," Baptiste said. *"C'est impossible."*

Oh dear, Belial said. *I may need to tell someone about this.*

Baptiste scuffled out from the chamber. In his right hand, he held a silver sword. In his left, he held a fraying leather thong, wrapped around the neck of a thick glass vial.

The vial held something dark.

As Baptiste held it up, it sloshed from side to side.

Natalie's scars tingled.

Belial sighed. *I was hoping he wouldn't find that.*

"No," Beth said, shaking her head. "No way. It can't be."

Baptiste held up the vial until it caught the light from the vehicles on the street outside. "Her sword," he murmured. "And her blood. No one dreamed it even existed."

"Is it?" Natalie asked.

For the life of the flesh is in the blood, and I have given it to you upon the altar to make an atonement for your souls.

"Why didn't you tell me there was more than just the sword?" she hissed.

How could I know it was still there?

"Is it?" Beth asked, turning to her.

Natalie nodded.

"Of course it is." Beth sighed. "Don't know why I even asked." As she spoke, she curled her feet under her. Then she brought one leg to her chest and splayed her fingers on the floor.

Natalie bit back a nervous smile. *My sister, the high-school track star.* She wanted to tell Beth she loved her, that even if Maillard's bullet burned straight through her heart, she'd force it to keep beating until she'd said those three words one more time.

A door slammed downstairs, almost directly beneath them. A man's voice shouted "Clear!"

The building had been evacuated. The bomb squad was getting closer.

"Take it," Baptiste said, passing the vial to Maillard. "*Gardez avec votre vie.*"

Maillard held up the cord to loop around his neck.

He's vulnerable, Belial said. *Go.*

Natalie launched herself toward Maillard.

CHAPTER TWENTY-FIVE

Malone Marchand clutched his wine glass. He smiled at Yves Collard, but his attention was focused on the raised voices outside the ballroom. They were faint, but he could still make them out — Baptiste and Doctor Brandon.

Her voice was raised, excited, angry.

His was lower pitched, a cornered animal growling a warning.

That wasn't like Baptiste. He was usually all bluster, bowling undergrads and administrators alike over with his reputation and his booming voice. Whatever she'd found to use as a verbal weapon had subdued him.

He wondered what the hell it was.

From the moment she'd walked into the ballroom, he'd been intrigued. He knew her by reputation, both from her books and her op-eds on higher education in the *New York Times*. Before he'd ever met her, he knew they would have a great deal in common. But he wasn't prepared for the effect she had on him in person. There were plenty of women in Paris with blonde hair, blue eyes, and shapely legs. But he hadn't met anyone with the same spark, the same combination of vulnerability and ferocity. It surrounded her with a halo, like a medieval saint in a Memling triptych.

And Baptiste was treating her like a second-class citizen.

It wasn't right.

And neither was he, for allowing it to happen.

"Excuse me for a moment, gentlemen," he said, ducking out of the group of presenters. He set his wine glass on the side table and strode out of the ballroom. Holding open the double doors, he glanced left and right in the ballroom's vestibule.

Everything had gone silent—no Baptiste, no Doctor Brandon.

So why hadn't anyone come back into the ballroom?

He let go of the doors and crossed the vestibule, into a dark hallway.

On the edge of the burgundy carpeting, near the baseboard, lay a lipstick and a minibar-sized bottle of vodka. He picked them up and glanced down the hallway. A large, dark figure scuffled through the door at the far end. The figure was off-balance and strangely disproportionate, like Quasimodo.

Marchand snapped his wrist to his jacket pocket for his glasses and held the lenses in front of his eyes.

Quasimodo hadn't escaped from bell tower of Notre Dame after all.

Baptiste was the hunchback, lumbering with a blonde figure slung over his shoulder. Her bag was wedged upside down between his ear and her torso, dropping items as they went.

Marchand reached for his phone.

CHAPTER TWENTY-SIX

Marius picked up the pike. Already he heard the sound of footsteps shuffling up the stairs from the sacristy. "Can you climb out the window?" he said to Léonie.

She shook her head. "I'm not hiding while you face them alone."

"Open the window." He pulled her behind him, aiming the pike toward the open door. "We'll climb out together."

A shout and a moan echoed from the garden below, followed by laughter and cheers.

Léonie splayed her fingers over the lead-glass window. There was no casement, no latch. "I could break it," she said, rotating the sword until the hilt faced the window.

Marius felt a claw of fear tear through his gut. If they broke the window, the murderers in the garden would look up and see them. They'd have to run along steep slate rooftops, keeping their footing as the sans-culottes tossed rocks and pikes at them. It was desperate and it probably wouldn't work, but it was the best hope they had. In this room, they could take no more than two or three of the sans-culottes before they were overwhelmed. "Do it," he said.

Léonie slammed the sword handle into the thick glass. It cracked, but did not splinter.

"Again," he said. Then he turned toward the door and took a deep breath. The pike felt solid in his hands, but he had no idea how to maneuver it. It would be only seconds now.

A dirty blond head poked around the doorframe. "What's going on here?" Brown eyes moved from Marius to the dead body on the floor, lying in a pool of blood. "You're traitors!" he said. "Traitors to the revolution!"

Léonie cried out as she struck the window again. A few shards flew over the sloped roof below.

"I have no wish to fight you," he said to the blond man. "Please let us leave in peace. We have done you no harm."

"You want to leave in peace?" The man came around the corner, an axe in his hand. "Then you must take the oath."

Marius pressed his lips. A bead of sweat rolled down the side of his face. "I cannot."

"Take the oath," the man said again, swinging the axe.

"No."

"Take the oath!" the man cried.

Léonie knocked out more of the glass with her third strike, and tried to clamber up onto the narrow window ledge.

"No." Marius stepped to the side, away from the body on the floor. If he tripped over it when he lashed out with the pike, he was dead. If he didn't stop the sans-culotte, Léonie was dead.

"A priest and a girl." The blond man tilted his head. "Almost doesn't seem fair."

Marius lunged. He stuck the pike into the other man's belly and let go, afraid to come closer, beneath the fall of his axe.

The man howled and gripped the pike with his left hand. Marius watched in horror as the man pulled it from his belly. A rush of dark blood streamed out. "What now, priest?" he said, grinning as his eyes glowed with bloodlust and anger.

Léonie jumped down from the window ledge, the sword clutched in her right hand. She whipped it around, blade pointing outward. Then she lunged with her right leg and drove it through the blond man's heart.

The man's arm fell. The blade of his axe caught her across the thigh as he dropped it. He looked at her with surprise as his grin faded to a grimace. She ripped out her sword and he fell to the floor, wide-eyed and ashen-faced.

Marius looked at her in awe. "I should have done that," he said. "You are so much braver than I."

She turned her back on the body still twitching beneath her. A few drops of blood had splattered across her cheeks. "Not braver," she said. "Just angrier."

He bent to pull the pike from the dead man's hand. "The window," he said. "Run."

Léonie frowned. "I won't leave you."

"You have to."

More footsteps scuffed up the stairs. Marius heard the jangling and clanking of chains, keys, and weapons. Another guttural cry sounded from the garden. The murderers roared their approval, shaking the broken pane in the window.

"You have to go," he said. "Or what was it all for?"

"For love," she said, touching his face. "What else?"

CHAPTER TWENTY-SEVEN

Maillard's eyes widened. He fumbled with the leather cord to get it over his head in time. Natalie plowed into him, grinding her shoulder into his solar plexus and reaching for his gun with both hands. The vial flopped against his chest, just above her head.

Maillard stumbled backward.

A flash of black streaked past her, trailing swear words in multiple languages. Beth had burst out of her runner's stance to charge Baptiste.

Maillard's left hand wound in her long hair and jerked her head back. The pain lit up her scalp the way Belial lit up the inside of her skull. It hurt, but she was used to it. *Try harder, asshole,* she thought, charging forward until Maillard's back hit the wall. She pushed on his wrist, slamming it to try and break his grip on the gun.

Maillard grunted and twisted the hand that held her hair.

Her scalp sizzled and her head snapped to the side. She lost her grip on his gun hand.

Then he swept his leg under her feet and let go of her hair. She felt herself falling.

Her fingers reached out for the vial of Joan's blood. He batted them away.

She hit the floor in front of the shrine, a prostrate supplicant to the blood of martyrs shed more than two hundred years ago. She turned her head, her field of vision filled with the brick-colored rivulets enclosed behind the shine's fragile glass. "Belial," she whispered. "What did you want me to see?"

Your six-times great-grandfather, the angel said.

CHAPTER TWENTY-EIGHT

SEPTEMBER 2, 1792
PARIS, FRANCE

His hands shook as they stood, side by side, weapons pointed at the door. There was no way out. These were the last minutes of his life.

Visions of an old age he would never have flashed before him like lightning — sitting in a garden, lifting his head to the springtime sun. Walking with the village children as they showed him a hive they'd found in a hollow tree. Complaining about his stiff joints in winter. The visions bled away into pictures of the life he had lived. The sweetness of his mother's onion tarts. The tingle of anticipation in his belly the first time he'd lectured to a classroom. And the clap of thunder in his heart the first time he saw Léonie, fierce and dirty in the tunnel.

I am not ready, he thought. *I want more.*

But greed was a sin, and he loved God as much as he knew how to love anyone or anything. He had only wanted to save Léonie, but now she would die, too. "Why won't you go?" he whispered, turning to her in the last moment before the jangling throng of sans-culottes ascended the stairs.

"I have nowhere to go but hell," she said.

"The God I love would never send you there."

Her stone-gray eyes blinked and two tears slipped down her cheeks. "It was good, wasn't it?"

He felt his own chin quiver. "Yes," he said. "It was good."

Four sans-culottes rounded the corner.

Marius shivered. The first was a long-haired man dressed in blue pants and a linen tunic painted red with five-finger splays. His hands were red, with a string of pink tubes wrapped around his left wrist. His eyes flickered over Léonie and he raised the axe in his hand.

Marius let out a roar and charged him with the pike.

The man grunted and sidestepped.

He tried to lever the pike around.

The man swung his axe sideways, slicing into Marius's midsection. A swath of fire tore through his entire body. He bent double and stumbled past him into the wall. A second man stepped out from behind the first. "My turn," the man said, stabbing a pike into his chest. He heard the tip scrape into the wall behind him. The man pulled it out and stabbed him again.

Behind them, Léonie swung her sword, slashing left and right at the man who approached her with a cuirass. Blade sparked on blade as Léonie shrieked, her beautiful face wracked with rage.

Her voice is right, Marius thought. *She will live.* Something warm spread through him, like sunlight. But before it reached his fingertips, it turned cold. He turned cold.

The man with the cuirass ducked and slashed at Léonie's thighs. She tried to block, but the blow was cast. Her tunic blossomed with red.

"Nothing for me?" the fourth sans-culotte said, whirling a small dagger in his hands.

"Finish her," the man with the cuirass said.

The coldness inside made him want to shiver. But he couldn't. The pike was holding him in place. *Close your eyes,* he told himself. *Do not watch her perish.*

He closed them.

The man holding the pike that was still inside him wriggled it. The pain was mercury in his veins, burning and freezing at the same time. "Open your eyes," the man growled. "Or I'll cut them out of your head."

Marius obeyed, wondering how fear could have a hold over him still. *I am a coward*, he thought. *I am hateful in the sight of the Lord.*

Léonie staggered back, both legs bent and bleeding. She clasped the sword with two hands, pointing it outward to keep her two attackers at bay. He could not bear to look at her face. He watched her hands, knuckles glowing, her left hand doused with blood.

But it was she who looked to him.

He felt it.

He felt her.

Seeking him, comforting him, loving him, with the force of will he still did not understand.

Marius lifted his eyes. *Let my last glimpse be of her,* he thought. Something warm and liquid filled his mouth. He thought it might choke him, so he opened his mouth.

Léonie held her sword low, waving it from side to side. The three men stepped closer, one foot at a time.

A man holding a pike thrust it at her. She jumped to the side, slashing out with her sword. One of the men howled, a slice of red opening up on his sleeve.

He wanted to reach out for her, but he couldn't move. The pike held him fast to the wall. He tried to say her name, but the word was caught in a thick bubble of blood. He would choke on it.

One of the men pulled back his hand.

He knew what would come next.

Marius forced the great bubble of blood up out of his throat. He spat it upon the sans-culotte in front of him to scream her name.

When the dagger struck her in the heart, he slumped forward, adrift in a sea of hopeless blackness.

CHAPTER TWENTY-NINE

Maillard pointed the gun at her, his finger curled around the trigger.

His father, Belial said. *Tell him his father is angry with him.*

Natalie's eyes flickered past Maillard, where Beth and Baptiste tangled in a flail of arms. Beth held Baptiste's right wrist with both hands, while he strained to keep the sword out of her reach.

Tell him! Belial shouted. He tapped her with a feather, igniting a wildfire on her temporal lobe.

"Your father is angry with you!" she shrieked.

"You're lying," Maillard hissed.

"He's trying to talk to you," she said, pushing herself up on her elbows. She had to get back on her feet. She had to help Beth. "He's telling Belial, who will tell me."

Maillard's eyebrow twitched. He adjusted his grip and fixed her in the pistol's sight.

"He's the reason you're doing this, isn't it? That's what you said in the chapel. You built your whole life around what happened to him. Don't you want to know what he's saying to you now?"

Maillard dropped to one knee and pressed the barrel of the gun to her forehead.

"Belial," she whispered. "Tell me."

Make him put the gun down first, the angel said.

Behind them, Beth pushed Baptiste over the threshold of the secret room. The back of Baptiste's head slammed into the five-foot doorway and he grunted. They disappeared into the room, still scrambling for control of the sword.

Natalie grimaced. *Help her, Belial*, she begged. *She needs you.*

I have killed in this room before. Did you know that, little one?

"What?"

Would you like me to do it again?

She looked at Maillard. Blond stubble darkened his cheeks and chin. Beads of sweat dripped down the sides of his face. Were Joan's relics worth dying for? A saint's blood couldn't save anyone from suicide bombers and rocket-propelled grenades. Was she any better than Baptiste if she killed Maillard now? "I don't know," she said.

A splintering crash from below echoed through the building. *The bomb squad*, she thought. *They're right below us.*

"Don't do this," she said to Maillard. "There must be something you still want in life."

"I want my father back," he said.

Be careful what you wish for, Belial replied.

A fierce wave of blackness washed over her. She scrambled into a sitting position, hands pressed to the floor. As she moved, the blackness dissolved into a foggy watercolor picture of a man — a man with the same golden eyes as Maillard. "I see him," she said. "He looks like you."

"You're lying." Maillard gripped her shoulder with his left hand.

"He's…" She turned her head, as if that would help her see what the blurry man was doing. "He's walking toward a fountain, in the center of an old square."

Maillard's grip felt like it would tear her muscle from the bone. "What does he say?"

The blurry man's lips began to move, but she could only hear the sound of her heartbeat thudding in her ears. "I can't hear," she said. "Belial, help me! I can't hear!"

Of course you can, the angel said. *You're just not listening.*

"I can't!" she cried, thrashing on the floor under Maillard. He would shoot her now. Then what would happen to Beth? It was all Belial's fault. Why was he promising things he couldn't deliver? Why wasn't he helping her?

From inside the tiny chamber, Beth screamed.

Then she screamed, envisioning a spray of her sister's blood.

The blurry man reached out a hand. His lips opened and shaped four words. "He wants to see you," she moaned, reaching out for Maillard the way his father reached out to her.

She grabbed his arm and clung to it. "He wants to see you," she sobbed. The blurry man was just saying it over and over, but now he was crying, just like her. Everything was blurry. Everything was foggy. Everything hurt. All she could see was a man, crying and waving toward a fountain.

"Get off me!" Maillard said. She felt him trying to shake her loose. He couldn't raise his arm as long as she clung to it. The blurry man didn't want her to let him go, though. The blurry man wanted her to —

She gasped. "No."

Maillard roared. With her clinging to his arm, he slammed it into the shrine.

The brittle glass broke over her back, showing her in shards.

The blurry man vanished in weeping watercolor trails.

Belial moaned.

She felt hot and cold all at once.

And then instead of the blurry man, she saw a man in a black robe. She saw him pinned to that very piece of plaster, held in place by a sword, the front of his robe torn and bloody.

Belial roared. *People do not judge in the same way as courts of law; they do not hand down sentences, they throw thunderbolts.*

"He's gone," she sobbed, but she didn't know if she meant Maillard's father or the black-robed man.

I did not want you to find out this way, the angel said. *That was never what I intended.*

She heard a click — Maillard's pistol.

She flung out her hands, as if they'd protect her from a bullet. "Your father was crying," she said, patting the air and trying to feel Maillard. "He didn't want you to do this. He wanted me to … he told me to …"

She couldn't say it. She dropped her hands to the floor to push herself up. Her right hand came down on a piece of jagged glass and she cried out with pain.

Do it, Belial said.

"What did he tell you?" Maillard asked.

Show him, Belial said. *Go on.*

CHAPTER THIRTY

Léonie *looked down* at her chest. A wooden handle protruded from it, bloody fingerprints smeared across the grain.

Oh, dear, the voice said. *That's unfortunate. Would you like help with that?*

But the voice didn't give her time to answer. Without her willing it, her hand reached up and pulled out the knife. Her fingers twirled the handle for a better grip and threw it into the throat of the man who'd stabbed her.

One down, the voice said calmly.

The man gasped and raised both hands to his throat. Over his shoulder, she saw it — Marius, slumped over a pike that pinned him to the wall, a stream of blood dribbling down his chin. One of the sans-culottes stood in front of him, still holding the pike.

"No!" she cried. She raised her right arm and slashed with Jeanne's sword. The voice wasn't helping her this time. Anger gave her strength and she pushed all thought of her bleeding legs from her mind. Marius's pain was all she could think of—and how none of the men in this room would ever leave it. "You killed him!" she cried. "You killed a good man!"

The man with the cuirass slashed at her again.

She raised her sword to block the blow.

The man with the pike reached back and threw. She spun like a dancer, arms tucked to her chest. The pike's point slammed into the stone wall, not her chest. As it clattered to the floor, she dropped into a crouch and swung the sword with all her strength. Her arm moved like a whisper. Was the voice helping her still? Jeanne's sword sliced the calves of the first man and the thighs of the second.

Both men howled. The man with the pike fell, holding a red hand over the pulse of blood seeping from his thigh.

She rose from her crouch, gripping the sword handle with both hands. "You fear me only now," she said, looking into the eyes of the first man. "You should have feared me the moment you laid eyes on me."

"Who are you?" the man on the floor said.

"Let the devil tell you."

The man with the cuirass roared and swung at her. If the blow caught her, it would lop off her head in a single stroke. She ducked, then bobbed to her full height and arced the sword to her right. His hand came off at the wrist.

The fourth man, the one holding Marius with the pike, spat at her. He pulled the pike out of her lover. She screamed to cover the sound as Marius's body slumped to the floor, blood and gouges staining the wall behind him. She kicked the handless man in the belly and thrust the tip of her sword into the pike-thrower's chest.

Two down, the voice said. *The third's not dead just yet.*

She thrust Jeanne's sword backward and toward the floor, embedding the tip in the third man's chest.

That's my girl, the voice said.

"Now it is you, and now it is me," she said, holding the gaze of the man who had killed Marius. She whirled the sword in her hand, refreshing her grip.

He charged.

His pike stabbed out at her, left then right. Jeanne's sword blocked his advance, but she couldn't press forward beneath his mighty hail of blows. She was afraid of the bodies on the floor — they'd trip her, throw off her precarious balance. Léonie felt the hot blood leaking down her right leg. Her eyes were leaking, too, as was her nose. Everything inside her was emptying. Did that mean the voice would leave her, too?

Stay, she pleaded. *Don't leave me.*

Never, the voice said. A prick of starlight burned behind her eyes. As her senses began to register the searing pain, her vision went black. All sensation dimmed, but she felt herself moving.

Not just moving … but standing tall, and striking with more force. *My soul is eclipsed*, she thought. *The devil has finally come for me.*

The clang of metal on metal thudded in her brain, dull like a distant memory, yet she knew it was happening right in front of her. *For behold*, the voice said, *the Lord cometh out of his place to punish the inhabitants of the earth for their iniquity.*

She felt her swings increase in speed. The devil was an excellent swordsman. He charged, feinted, plucked her feet up and over the corpses on the ground, until together they had trapped Marius's killer in the far corner of the room.

What would you like me to tell him before he dies? the voice — no, the devil — asked.

He allowed her to turn her head for a moment to look down at Marius. Blood pooled beneath his lifeless body. Red-stained hands clutched at the wounds in his chest. His eyes and mouth were open. "You killed the only good man I have ever known. May there be no pity for you in this life or the next."

The devil repeated her words. Then he raised her right arm and brought Jeanne's sword down across the murderer's neck, nearly severing his head. When the body fell to the floor, she pushed it aside with her foot. She wanted no part of it to touch Marius. The devil, being the devil, translated her push into a swift kick.

"No!" she shouted. But the words echoed inside her closed mouth. "Let me go!"

I don't think that's in your best interest right now. You're barely alive.

"I don't care," she said.

You will, the devil said. *And stop calling me the devil. I'm the furthest thing from it. Someday you'll understand that.*

"Do it," she said.

A cold wind swept through her. Suddenly, she could see and move and speak — and hurt. Her sword arm fell to her side and she crumpled to her knees. She looked down at her right leg, where the first slash had caught her. The stream of blood flowed like the Seine after a storm.

Léonie gasped.

Blood.

The vial.

She forced her left hand to press against her chest, feeling for the outline of the vial. If it was intact, she hadn't failed entirely. Her fingers, strange lumps of lead attached to her hands, finally managed to clasp the glass and she sobbed with relief. Mother Marie-Aimée had given her a task, and she would complete it.

She looked toward the secret chamber. Its door was open.

"You will help me if I need it," she growled to the devil. "Do you understand?"

But the voice did not answer.

For the first time in many years, she was alone.

She sucked in her breath and began to crawl across the room, dragging the sword in her right hand. The pain in her leg was too great to stand. If she tried, she suspected she would faint. A great smear of blood trailed behind her. From the chapel below, she heard cries and jeers and sobs. *This is not a church,* she thought. *It is a slaughterhouse.* How could anyone, even God, cleanse this place of its madness?

She crawled over the threshold of the secret chamber and pulled herself toward the stone box in the far corner. Her arms burned and shook with each stroke. She swore out loud, urging herself forward with every curse. Finally, she propped herself against the wall and panted. The sweat that dripped from her limbs was cold, as if she were already dead.

With a ragged breath, she lifted the lid from the box and placed Jeanne's sword in its hiding place. One hand reached beneath her robe and pulled the leather cord that held the vial of Jeanne's blood. Gently, with a shaking hand, she set it beside the sword.

"I did it," she whispered, touching her fingers to her lips and then to the sword. "I love you, *maman*." A tear slipped down her cheek at the memory of Marie-Aimée. She brushed it away and shivered. Now it wasn't just her sweat that was cold. Her skin was icy, too.

There was only one thing left to be done.

She crawled out of the room and stared at the stone door. She would have to push it closed, but neither her arms nor legs had the strength to move. *I can't do it*, she thought. *I'm dying.*

She turned away with a sob. Marius lay not two meters from her, his eyes still open. Still watching her. *He died for me*, she thought. *He died to try and protect me.*

An alchemy of fury and love drove her to her feet. She put all her weight on her right side and limped toward the door. With a sob, she pressed it closed.

Then, as stars burst and faded before her eyes, she fell to the floor and crawled toward Marius, her only remaining desire to die in his arms.

CHAPTER THIRTY-ONE

"*I don't want* to," Natalie whispered.

You don't want to save yourself? Belial snapped. *What about your sister? Baptiste is about to send that sword into her heart, you know.*

"No!" Her blood raced with panic and adrenaline. She couldn't see anything. All she knew was that Maillard's pistol was still pressed to her forehead ... and that in her vision, his father had asked for something terrible.

"What did he say?" Maillard's voice boomed. "Tell me or you die."

If he wanted to kill her, even Belial couldn't stop him. The gun's muzzle velocity would be around 300 meters per second. An angel's was ... less. There was no choice but to do what he asked. She splayed the fingers of both hands on the floor beside her.

"Belial," she said. "Let me see him."

The angel bent his head and folded his wings. The watercolor blackness behind her eyelids began to fade. She saw a pale slash of color that materialized into Maillard's face … and the gun pressed to her forehead. His finger was already wrapped around the trigger.

"You'll kill me whether I tell you or not," she said.

"Yes." He clenched the muscles of his jaw.

"Let my sister go. She'll name Baptiste, but not you."

"Tell me now or I kill you both."

Natalie gulped. The only thing she had left to bargain with was the truth.

She turned the full weight of her pale-eyed stare on him. "I saw him," she said. "He was walking toward a fountain. It was someplace he knew. Someplace he'd been happy."

Maillard shuddered.

"There was a coin in his hand, and he twirled it between his fingers."

His arm began to droop.

"He held it out to me, and told me to throw it in the fountain. He said to make a wish, and if I did, he'd tell me what he wished for."

The gun was pointed at her chest now.

She let the fingers of her right hand spider-walk over the floor until they found a triangular shard of glass. "So I made my wish," she said, pausing. "And I leaned over and whispered it into your father's ear. I told him I wished for my sister to live. He smiled at me, and he leaned toward me to tell me his wish."

Maillard's Adam's apple bobbed as he swallowed thickly.

"His wish was for you." Her fingers rocked the shard upright. She stabbed her hand over the top of the triangle, embedding it like a sail on the ocean of her palm. Her eyes filled with tears, but she didn't know if it was because of the pain in her hand or the pain in her heart. "But you knew that, didn't you?"

Maillard's hand shook and he leaned forward. The muzzle of the gun drooped toward her elbow.

"He wished that you ... "

She took a breath, as if to speak. Then she slashed out with her right hand. A thin red line opened on his throat. She tucked her arms to her chest and rolled toward the shrine.

Maillard pulled the trigger. The bullet tore into the floor.

"Natalie!" Beth screamed from inside the hidden chamber.

She raised her feet and kicked, catching Maillard in the groin. He bent toward her with a groan and fired again. The shot whizzed past her ear.

She scrambled to her feet and leapt behind Maillard. This time, she slapped her palm onto the back of his neck. The glass sank deep into his skin.

His left arm flailed behind him, reaching for her. She tried to pull her hand from his neck, but the glass was stuck. She screamed and jerked her hand free, splashing a trail of blood across the floor.

In the secret chamber, metal scraped against stone. Sparks lit up the darkness.

"Beth!" she cried.

Not yet, Belial said.

She whirled to check Maillard's position. The glass triangle stuck out from the back of his neck, but he was rising to his feet.

He would shoot her in a quarter-turn.

She hurled herself at him head-first. Her weight struck him in the hip and they fell backward together. His amber eyes met hers, widening in fear as he crashed to the ground.

The shard of glass burst through his neck, a guillotine blade in reverse.

He gasped and reached out for her throat. "My father," he sputtered. "*Mon père.*"

"He was ashamed of what you've become," she said. "He wished you were dead."

She flung his hand away as the light faded from his eyes.

CHAPTER
THIRTY-TWO

ell was not what she'd expected. Uncomfortable, yes. But bumpy? Léonie had never guessed that the devil's realm would feel so much like a wagon rolling over rutted cobblestones. The amount of pain she felt seemed right for hell, though. Her entire body ached. She couldn't identify whether she felt hot or cold. Everything was one searing black ball of lumpy, bumpy pain.

Suddenly, the last moments of her life came flooding back to her. The hidden chamber, the sword, the vial, the men … and Marius.

Where was he?

With her last breath, she'd lifted his arm from the floor and pushed her shoulders under it, safe for all eternity in his embrace.

But of course he wouldn't be in hell.

So she'd been sent here alone.

She'd expected it, of course, but there'd always been a tiny shred of hope, flickering like a candle in a gust of wind. Until the end, she'd never killed anyone. She'd never lied to anyone. But she'd been so angry, at the world and the voice and then at the man who pinned Marius to the wall.

If I don't open my eyes, she thought, *I'll never know he's not beside me.*

He's not beside you, the voice said.

Anger flooded her veins.

Open your eyes, it said. *You must flee this place.*

But I'm dead, she thought.

You have a reason to live.

Something sharp poked her and she gasped.

Now, the voice said, its tone growing louder, like a father angry with his daughter.

The jolting movement continued and she almost opened her eyes just to see if hell really was an endless ride on an unpaved road.

That's right, the voice said. *Just open your eyes.*

There was another jolt. Something hard slammed into her leg. The pain sizzled like a burst of flame.

Léonie opened her eyes.

The sun was hot upon her face. All around her lay the bloodied arms and faces and legs of the men inside the church. The air smelled of offal and refuse. She felt the bile rise to her throat and tried to push herself up to her elbows.

Shops and taverns and stables jolted by, visible over a wooden rail. *I am in a cart*, she thought. Panic drove her upright, giving her strength even as her bloody hands slipped over and through the tangled clutch of limbs around her.

"No," she moaned, feeling the bile surge toward her teeth.

Her right leg wouldn't respond when she pressed on it.

Out, she thought. *I want out.*

Would you like my help? the voice asked.

Léonie remembered the dim sensations that had reached her when he took control of her, killing the sans-culottes. It would be so easy to let go, to let him take away her ability to feel pain and smell death. But she didn't trust him.

She sank her lip into her teeth and clamped down. Then she forced her bleeding leg to bend. Pain flew through her body with wings of fire. But she moved, centimeter by centimeter, toward the rear of the cart.

The dead were being taken to the cemetery. They would be dumped into a pit and covered with quicklime. She'd heard Mother Marie-Aimée make the arrangements when smallpox swept through the convent. Four sisters had died. Marie-Aimée had sent for the grave digger, who drove a cart like this one.

You will not bury me, she thought, dangling her legs over the open back of the cart.

It wobbled at a slow, steady pace. There was nothing for it but to fling herself off and fall against the cobbles. If she cried out, they would find her.

I will catch you, the voice said as she pushed with her arms.

Her body fell to the ground.

Something in her leg crunched. A bone, perhaps.

Her arms seemed to work, though. She clamped her teeth onto her right fist to keep from crying out.

The grave digger did not look back.

Léonie watched the cart pull away, its cargo bruised and bloody and in pieces. Here a head. There a torso with no arms. Blood everywhere. The vile smells of violated bodies wafted toward her and this time, she did vomit.

Only then did she realize Marius was somewhere among the tangle of bodies in that cart.

"Put me back," she whispered, pulling herself toward it.

I cannot, the voice said. *My job is to ensure you survive, despite your best efforts.*

The stack of bodies swayed with the movement of the cart. Limbs smacked gently against other limbs. They were all beyond pain now.

"Put me back! I belong with him."

You belong with me.

She had no strength to argue. Her arms shook, refusing to hold her up against the cobbles.

Crawl out of the way before another cart runs you over. We will tend to your wounds later.

Let the devil tend them, she thought. *I'll see him soon enough.*

CHAPTER THIRTY-THREE

Maillard's head lolled to the side. Beside it, the vial of Joan's blood lay shattered, broken during their fight. Natalie ignored it, pushing herself to her feet and stumbling toward the secret chamber.

Inside, Beth and Baptiste clutched the handle of Jeanne's sword, each trying to rip it from the other's grasp. Her sister's back was to her, but Baptiste saw her enter. The whites of his eyes widened. "Let it go," she said to him. "It's over."

He bared his teeth at her and wrenched both arms to the right.

Beth stumbled but held her grip on the sword.

"Okay, you asked for it." She strode toward him and reached out with her bleeding hand.

Baptiste scuffled into a corner, trying to protect his back. Beth stumbled along with him, strong enough to hold the sword but not strong enough to pry it from his grip.

"Just a few more seconds," she said, sliding past Beth.

Baptiste kicked out at her, but couldn't do more without letting go of the sword. She sucked in her breath and moved closer to him. His foot connected with her shin and she hissed. She turned sideways and pushed with her hip, sliding herself into the corner behind him.

Baptiste flung his weight back, slamming her into the stone wall. The force of his movement shook the sword from Beth's grip. Her sister shrieked and jumped backward as Baptiste swung the sword at her.

"No!" Natalie cried. Her body was pinned, but her arms were free. She reached around his head and dug her fingers into his eyes.

Baptiste roared and bent forward, pulling out of her grip.

It was all the distraction Beth needed. She ducked and grabbed for the sword, tearing it from his grip. "Fucker," she said, panting.

Natalie slid out from behind Baptiste. Blood from her right palm streaked his cheek like crimson tears. He stood up and sank into his knees, fists clenched, as if he were about to charge.

"Go ahead," she said, pointing at Beth. "Give her a thrill."

Beth tightened her grip on the sword.

She slunk past Beth to grab the pistol Baptiste had set down in order to remove the sword.

"Maillard!" Baptiste called. His voice echoed in the small chamber.

"He's dead."

Baptiste caught his breath. His fists slowly unclenched as he realized what that meant.

Belial moved his wing a hair's breadth from her skull — a caress. *You killed a Légionnaire, little one. I'm impressed.*

"I'll kill anyone who threatens my family," she said.

"Come on." Beth backed out of the chamber, still pointing the sword at Baptiste. She sidestepped Maillard's body, using her toe to slide the pistol from his grip and then across the room. "I think the Sûreté will be interested in what you've been up to."

"They will agree with me," Baptiste hissed. "We have the same enemy."

"Sanity?" Beth said.

Baptiste's eyes fluttered over Natalie. "As if you two know what that means."

"My sister knows what's right, and no one could ever make her choose a different path. I don't know anything saner than that."

"Go," Natalie said, transferring the gun to her left hand. Her right was too slick with blood. She pointed it at Baptiste and he stumbled out of the chamber, gasping when he saw the glass protruding from Maillard's neck.

You can't be here much longer, little one, Belial said.

"I know." She followed Baptiste back out into the room. "The bomb squad's coming, Beth. How are we going to explain this?"

"We tell the truth," Beth said. "We haven't done anything wrong."

Her eyes flickered over Maillard's body. "I did."

"Self-defense is not a crime."

"Belial wants us to go."

"I'm not running." Beth shook her head. "We had help in Russia. We don't have anyone he —" Then she gasped and reached into her pocket, pulling out a business card. "Marchand," she whispered. "Nat, we need to find a phone."

"Take his," she said, jerking her right thumb at Baptiste. A thin stream of blood splashed against the wall.

"Your hand!" Beth gasped. "Let me see that."

"It can wait."

"The hell it can." Her sister slid the card back into her pocket. With Joan's sword in her right hand, Beth's left reached for her wounded palm. "You sliced through your lifeline? Jesus, Nat, go easy on the symbolism, okay?"

Baptiste backed toward the door.

"Stop," Natalie said, raising her left arm. "I'm losing blood, not brain cells."

"It won't work," he said softly. "Your American melting pot. You've infected the world with cowardice and called it tolerance."

"Want to prove how brave you are? You versus a bullet. Go."

"You wouldn't do it."

"But I would," Beth said, raising the sword. "So help me, I'll put this thing through you. Have fun with sepsis."

Sepsis. She looked down at the vial of blood, broken on the floor next to Maillard's body. She knelt beside it and pulled the leather cord from around his neck, a jagged piece of centuries-old glass attached to the top. "Was it really hers, Belial?"

It is not her blood I brought you to see, the angel said.

"I know," she whispered. "The shrine."

Behind the broken glass, the original wall fragment remained unharmed. Her eyes followed the trail of blood to its origin, the dark scrape dug into the limestone. That was all that was left of a human being, after a life lived in piety and a death that should never have happened. A dusty shrine, locked away from the world. It turned everything that had happened into nothing, as if he had never been born. She reached out and touched the fragment of limestone, letting her fingers slide down the bloodstains.

"Who was he?" she asked.

I told you, Belial answered.

Voices and the scuffle of footsteps sounded from the staircase down the hall.

"They're coming," Beth said.

She pressed harder against the wall fragment. It seemed impossible that the blood that stained the wall flowed in her veins. That he had been here, in the same chapel, in this very room. That he had died to protect Joan's sword and Joan's blood.

And something else, Belial said. The angel's voice was raw, as if he had been crying.

"Léonie," Natalie whispered. "He died to protect her, didn't he?"

He was a good man, little one, but I couldn't save him.

Beth put a hand on her shoulder. "Nat, I need you to focus."

She heard voices outside the door. Things that jangled. Something that smelled like smoke.

He is a part of you, Belial said. *And he never knew it. I had to save her. I didn't have time to tell him.*

The angel's shoulders shook with sobs.

She cried out as every one of his feathers stroked her skull. Now the tears were in her eyes, too, blurring the shrine and the limestone and the blood. There were only shards of glass, poisoned with her reflection.

The door burst open, kicked down by a man in black. Three men behind him swept into the room.

Beth dropped the sword and held up both hands. "My sister needs medical attention," she said. "She cut herself."

One of the black-clad men picked her up around the waist and pulled her away from the shrine. *Sleep now, little one,* Belial said, dropping her into unconsciousness as the man lifted her into his arms.

CHAPTER THIRTY-FOUR

Nicolas de Haldat du Lys lived in a small house just beyond the tavern. Léonie shivered as she trudged toward it, sidestepping a drunken man who stumbled out the tavern door. It was dark, but she drew the hood of her black cloak closer to her face. She wanted no one to be able to say they had seen her.

She forced her limbs to take the last few steps.

The house appeared empty. No candlelight shone through the two front windows. She took a deep breath and knocked her broken knuckles against the door.

Nothing happened.

The thought of walking any more tonight made her want to cry. Better, she thought, to collapse on this doorstep and wait for someone to remove her — a doctor, or if she waited long enough, an undertaker.

The sob burst from her throat just as the heavy door swung open.

Léonie looked up at a long face with a sharp nose and deep-set eyes. *"B — bonsoir, monsieur,"* she said. The word "citoyen" would never roll from her tongue, not without another knife in her breast. *"Je m'appelle — "*

The man leaned out the doorway and looked past her. "Are you alone out here? What happened to you?" He reached around her shoulders and guided her over the threshold. She limped as best she could, dragging her right leg behind her. The wound in her thigh had not healed, despite the kindness of several strangers.

He closed the door behind her and she breathed in the warm smell of roast chicken and rosemary. The scar on her chest ached with the deepness of her breath.

"Please sit," he said, gripping her shoulders with one hand and pulling a chair toward her with the other. She sank into it gratefully, moaning with relief when the cracked soles of her feet no longer had to hold her weight.

He lifted the chair, with her in it, and marched it across the room to the hearth. A black kettle hung from a hook over the fire. Her mouth watered so quickly she was afraid she would choke on her own saliva.

"Is there someone I can fetch for you?" He looked her up and down. "I have not seen you in the village before."

"I c — came from Paris."

His brown eyes dropped to her feet, wrapped in blood-soaked rags. "On foot?"

She nodded. The heat from the fire was so delicious she could barely speak. "Nicolas de Haldat du Lys," she said softly, meeting his gaze with hers. "Is that your name?"

He nodded, revealing no surprise.

"She told me to find you if anything went wrong."

"Who told you that?"

"The Reverend Mère, Marie-Aimée de Jésus." As she spoke the name, her eyes filled with tears. No matter how many times she cried, they always filled again. "They killed her. She asked something of me, and I could not do it." She reached beneath her cloak and untied the string of silver beads from her ceinture. "This is all I have left."

Nicolas curled her hand around the beads. "We heard about the massacres. When no letter arrived from her afterward ... "

He sighed and stood up. On the sideboard, a small collection of bowls and plates were stacked neatly. He picked up a bowl and spooned hot broth from the kettle into it. "Here," he said, holding it in front of her.

Léonie took the bowl and held it to her lips. The liquid, rich and salty, stung her chapped skin. She ignored the pain; she'd gotten used to that. "Thank you," she said between gulps. "It tastes so good I want to cry."

"When you're done with that, I'll get you some meat. If you could see yourself..."

"I'm sorry." She looked at the floor. "I had nowhere else to go."

"That's not what I meant." He held up a hand, as if he wanted to touch her cheek. "You look half-starved."

She nodded, trying to remember the last time she had tasted meat.

"Tell me about my aunt. You were at the convent with her?"

"She entrusted me with two things before she died. I was to carry them out of Paris. I failed her." She glanced up at him over the rim of the bowl, wondering if anyone other than Marie-Aimée knew the secret.

Nicolas raised one dark eyebrow. "What happened to these … things?"

"You know about them?"

"She didn't tell you who we are, did she?"

Léonie shook her head.

Nicolas smiled. "There are few who remember what our name means, and I intend to keep it that way. I doubt even my aunt could have recited the precise genealogy." He stood by the hearth, placing both hands on the mantel, his back to her. "Jeanne d'Arc had three brothers, each of whom had at least one child. A daughter married an uncle. A granddaughter married a cousin. Hundreds of years go by, and here I am." He turned his head toward her. "We kept Jeanne's sword and her blood with us until Marie-Aimée told us they would be safer with her, in Paris."

"But she told me she was born in Reims."

Nicolas nodded. "Daughters marry and move away. Her mother left, but never forgot."

"I ruined everything," she whispered. "I'm sorry."

"Hush," Nicolas said. "No more of that."

"They are still there, hidden in the convent. A man was going to help me carry them out. But…"

Nicolas's eyes took in her stained cloak, bandage-shod feet, and dried bloodstains on the skirt and bodice of her stolen dress. "They did these things to you?"

"Yes."

"How did you know where to find me?"

Do not tell him about me, the voice said.

"Your aunt told me." She offered a weak smile. "I have a good memory."

He held out his hands and she placed the empty bowl in them. "There is much I want to ask about what you have seen. But you look as if you'll fall asleep if I say another word."

"I've forgotten what it's like to feel warm."

"Is there somewhere you will be missed?"

"No," she whispered.

"Then you will stay until you are healed."

She glanced around the room, suddenly realizing how quiet the house was. No children, no elderly bones resting by the fire, no women sewing by candlelight. "Do you live alone?"

"I will be glad of the company." He stood up and made his way toward her, towering over her chair. "Shall I carry you?"

Léonie shook her head. "I walked here, didn't I?"

"That's no reason for you to walk any further." He slipped one arm around her back and another under her knees. When he picked her up, she let her head fall against his shoulder.

He will be good to you, the voice said. *And to your child.*

Léonie opened her eyes.

Oh, yes, the voice said. *Didn't you know?*

§

As she lay in bed, drifting off to a sleep she craved and dreaded, she asked the question she had never asked before. "Who are you?"

I am an angel.

"I thought you were a curse. A madness set upon me. I wanted to be rid of you."

I know.

"But you saved me." One hand slipped down to cradle her belly. "You saved us."

And I will do it again, if need be.

"What you did in that room … it was not me. No curse could do that."

Is that all I had to do to convince you?

"And you were the one who guided me here."

I have always had your best interests at heart.

"Why?"

There are those whom my master wishes to protect.

"Why?"

I cannot answer every question of yours. There are things even I do not know.

"Once, all I wanted was to be rid of you," she whispered.

And now?

"Promise me you will stay."

I have no wish to leave you.

"Forever," she added. "Stay with my baby, and my baby's baby. I could not bear to bring it into this world to face the cruelty that has been shown me."

The voice sighed, happy at last. *I swear it shall be done.*

CHAPTER THIRTY-FIVE

Natalie picked at the plastic tape that fixed a gauze bandage to her skin. The bomb squad had come with an ambulance in tow, and a med-tech had patched her up on the spot. She was supposed to go to the hospital for a scan, to make sure the smack on the stairs hadn't caused a fracture or any internal bleeding. The cut on her palm would heal, he'd said, as long as she left the butterfly bandages in place.

"Butterfly bandage," she said. "What a stupid name."

"I don't care what they call it if it works," Beth said. In the darkness, strobed with the flashing lights of French emergency vehicles, her sister looked like an artist's sketch — a white paper face, with charcoal dragged beneath her eyes and cheekbones.

Across the courtyard, a blue-suited policeman bundled Baptiste into the back seat of a Peugeot. His eyes narrowed with anger, directed at Beth. Her sister smiled and flipped him off.

"You're awfully calm," she said.

"I learned something after Russia." Her sister exhaled and smiled. "Be grateful for every breath."

"I killed someone. I feel like shit."

You should be proud of that, Belial said. *But you should never have handed over the sword.*

"It belongs to Joan," she said. "And Joan belongs to France."

"Babe," Beth said, turning her back on the fleet of emergency vehicles. "That reminds me. You never told me why Belial brought you here in the first place. If it wasn't Joan's sword, what was it?"

She looked into her sister's wide blue eyes. The blood in the shrine belonged to her six-times great-grandfather, too. She wanted to tell Beth what he had given them, but didn't know how to begin. She had nothing, not even a name. "I'll tell you," she said. "I just need some time."

"How about a hint?" Beth squeezed her shoulder gently. "Just one."

"Just one," she whispered back. "Genealogy."

Beth's eyes widened. Before she could reply, a French-accented voice shouted her name into the darkness. A handsome man with dark hair waved at them from behind the police perimeter. "Monsieur Marchand!" Beth called, waving back.

"Who's that?" Natalie asked.

"He's no fan of Baptiste, I can tell you that. I didn't know who else to call for help." Her sister blushed. "Turns out, he followed Baptiste out of the ballroom when I didn't come back."

"Go," she said, pushing Beth toward him. "I need a minute here alone."

"You sure you're all right?"

Natalie nodded. "For now."

"Don't go anywhere, okay? I'll be right back." Beth hurried toward the police tape. Marchand's face lit up at the sight of her. He reached for her hands as soon as she was near enough to touch.

You will need him someday, Belial said. *Perhaps more than she will.*

She let her eyes drift over his frame, from the broad shoulders to the strong hands clasping Beth's in his. She knew she should pay attention to where he put his hands and whether Beth tucked her hair behind her ear when she talked to him. But her heart was too sore to let anyone else in. All she could think of was the blood shrine, and the man who had died to save her six-times great-grandmother. "Start talking," she growled.

The French medic glanced at her and frowned. "Not you," she added.

I never meant for this to happen, the angel said. *I only wanted you to meet him.*

"Who was he?"

His name was Marius Landry. He was a priest and a teacher, a member of La Salle's Christian Brothers.

"You were there? During the massacre?"

I saw him die, the angel said. *I helped her live.*

"Who was she?"

Léonie, your six-times great-grandmother. One of the bravest women I've ever known.

"Were you…with her? The way you're with me?" A sharp feeling pierced her heart. When she realized what it was, she scraped her cheek against her shoulder to hide her face. "I thought you were mine."

I am, Belial said.

"How long have you been with…people?"

I will never leave you, little one.

"I know. I've asked politely and I've tried to kill myself and nothing worked."

I made her a promise.

"And who is she that you'd actually keep it?"

I belong to you and your descendants.

"Like I'll have any."

Oh, you're quite wrong.

"Never." Her fingers fumbled in her pocket, where she'd shoved the leather thong and broken glass vial. The medic hadn't found it when he looked her over, much to her surprise. If it had really been Joan's blood, she wanted to keep it…to remember what a girl who heard voices could achieve. "I wouldn't wish you on anyone."

But the angel didn't listen. He shook his feathers, knowing it would cause her knees to buckle and shake. *You will listen,* he said.

"No, I won't." She wrapped her fingers around the glass vial. She had no alcohol to slow him down, but she wondered if she could make herself drunk on pain. She could slice through the pads of each of her fingers with the broken vial. How much damage could she do before the medic caught on?

The angel fought back. She felt a shadow fall over her bones from the inside, its invisible weight holding her arm down when she fought to pull it up.

More than one man will love you, he said.

"I don't believe you."

One of them will give his life for you.

"Shut up."

And one of them will give you a daughter.

Natalie gasped. Her concentration broke and Belial won their tug-of-war. Her fingers let go of the vial. "You're lying."

We shall see, little one. We shall see.

The End

Author's Note

Thank you so much for reading! If you enjoyed the story, I'd really appreciate a brief review on Goodreads or your favorite book vendor's website — even a quick star rating can help get the word out. Your support means the world to me!

What Inspired this Book?

It's a single photo in an old issue of National Geographic. It's the July 1989 issue, celebrating the bicentennial of the French Revolution. I was only twelve years old at the time, but that photo was unforgettable. It's stayed with me for almost thirty years now. That picture is of the blood shrine. You can see it on the book's Pinterest board at https://www.pinterest.com/jenniwiltz/the-carmelite-prophecy/.

What's Real...and What's Not?

Most of the details about the massacre in Saint-Joseph-des-Carmes are real. The blood in the shrine is said to have come from a sword or pike used in the massacre, rested against the wall when the killer paused for a moment.

Marius and Léonie are entirely fictional, as is the secret chamber and the vial of Joan of Arc's blood. The sword Joan retrieved from the church dedicated to St. Catherine in Fierbois is lost to history. It may or may not be the same sword carried by Charles Martel – it's a beautiful legend, but it can't be proved.

Joan of Arc's brothers and their descendants did keep some of her effects, including a sword. Joan used several swords, though, and the documentation is spotty, so we can't be sure which sword they kept. No matter which one it was, it's said to have disappeared during the chaos of the revolution.

Want to Know When the Next Book Comes Out?
Sign up for my mailing list at http://jenniwiltz.com. There's a secret website page for subscribers that has a welcome video from me to you, plus free short story downloads. Readers like you are an inspiration and I'd love to hear from you. Email me anytime at jenni@jenniwiltz.com.

Until next time!

The Natalie Brandon Thrillers

BOOK 1: THE ROMANOV LEGACY
A MURDERED TSAR. A MISSING TREASURE.
ONE WOMAN HOLDS THE KEY.

Natalie Brandon knows Nicholas II, the last Russian tsar, left behind a secret bank account to provide for his family in exile. But getting someone to believe her is harder than finding the account itself.

Diagnosed with schizophrenia, Natalie is haunted by a recurring hallucination, the voice of an angel named Belial. Even her sister, a history professor, won't take her claim seriously…until a Russian spy kidnaps Natalie, claiming she's the only one who can lead him to the treasure.

But Russia's prime minister, Maxim Starinov, will do anything to get to it first. He joins the deadly hunt, ensnaring Natalie's sister, Constantine's partner, and a loyal Russian family whose only mission is to guard the Romanovs' secret. With her ghostly intuition guiding them, Natalie and Constantine must fight to save the tsar's legacy from a greedy despot.

BOOK 3: THE SINNER'S BIBLE
A CURSE TAKES HOLD WHEN
FAITH AND LOVE FALTER.

Natalie Brandon doesn't believe in curses – except for the one that's afflicting her.

Diagnosed with schizophrenia, Natalie is haunted by a recurring hallucination, the voice of an angel named Belial. When her boss acquires a copy of the rare 1631 Sinner's Bible, Belial tells her that the book is linked to the tragic Stuart dynasty – and the curse that brought it down.

Natalie doesn't believe it until the public unveiling of the book goes horribly awry. A pair of thieves take Natalie, her sister, and her boss hostage. When Belial orders her to keep the thieves from stealing the Sinner's Bible, Natalie knows it's because he wants to unleash the curse once more. Will she stop the thieves or will she stop Belial? No matter which choice she makes, someone will die.

ALL AVAILABLE IN DIGITAL AND PAPERBACK

Readers love the Natalie Brandon thrillers:
"believable and enchanting"
"wildly entertaining, very well written,
highly inventive, and just plain fun"
"a wonderful blend of history and mystery"

Also by Jenni Wiltz

THE RED ROAD
(LITERARY FICTION)

Emma's dad has always promised to send her to college. But when an act of gang violence almost takes his life, Emma can't move on. Will she do what he wants and focus on her own future…or will she jeopardize everything to seek revenge? Available in digital and paperback.

A VAMPIRE IN VERSAILLES
(HISTORICAL HORROR)

Jean-Gabriel de Bourbon is a vampire whose survival is tied to the French royal family. As long as a king sits on the French throne, Jean-Gabriel lives. But the year is 1788, and the French Revolution draws near. Is anyone, even a vampire, strong enough to stop the force of destiny? Available in digital and paperback.

I NEVER ARKANSAS IT COMING
(MYSTERY)

Brett Sargent isn't adapting to life in Arkansas very well. A native New Yorker in the Witness Protection Program, she's trying to keep a low profile after testifying against a Mafia up-and-comer. But when a Little Falls truck driver turns up dead with a Mafia calling card stabbed to his chest, Brett knows she's next on their hit list. Available in digital and paperback.

ABOUT THE AUTHOR

Author photo by Ryan Donahue

Jenni Wiltz writes fiction and creative nonfiction. She's won national writing awards for her short fiction, romantic suspense, and creative nonfiction. Her short stories have appeared in *Gargoyle*, the *Portland Review*, and an anthology published by the *Chicago Tribune*. When she's not writing, she enjoys running and genealogical research. She lives in Pilot Hill, California. Visit her online at JenniWiltz.com.

www.ingramcontent.com/pod-product-compliance
Lightning Source LLC
Chambersburg PA
CBHW050356190726
48284CB00007BB/2306